Look what people are saying about Tori Carrington...

"Warning needed: Whatever you do—just buy the book!
Do not try to read parts in a public place!
This one is seriously, seriously, passionately hot!
An absolute sizzler!"
—*freshfiction.com* on *Shameless*

"Tori Carrington is an unparalleled storyteller with
an imagination that is absolutely matchless.
These authors are extraordinary and have a
true gift for putting their own special brand
on anything they touch."
—*Rendezvous* on *Private Investigations*

"One of the genre's most beloved authors."
—*Rendezvous*

"Smart, sassy, and sizzling!"
—Robin Peek, *WordWeaving.com*

"Outrageously hot and erotic."
—Diana Tidlund, *WritersUnlimited.com*

"Deliciously delightful."
—*SimeGen.com*

"A blazing triumph..."
—Harriet Klausner

"One of category's most talented authors."
—*EscapetoRomance.com*

Blaze™

Dear Reader,

You've heard them. The songs that stick in your head and refuse to go away no matter what you do. If you were to make a list, Rick Springfield's "Jessie's Girl" would rank in the Top Ten, no doubt. So it was only natural that we'd end up writing a book tailor-made to fit the song at some point. The second title in our *Indecent Proposals* miniseries is that book.

In *Reckless*, sexy caterer Heidi Joblowski is convinced her longtime boyfriend's best friend, hottie architect Kyle Trapper, hates her. But Kyle doesn't hate her—he's secretly in lust with her. A secret that Kyle's finding harder and harder to keep under wraps the more time he spends around Heidi. The problem? She's his best friend Jesse's girl.

We hope you enjoy every tryst and turn of Heidi and Kyle's journey toward happily-ever-after. We'd love to hear what you think. Contact us at P.O. Box 12271, Toledo, OH 43612 (we'll respond with a signed bookplate, newsletter and bookmark), or visit us on the Web at www.toricarrington.net.

Here's wishing you love, romance and *hot* reading.

Lori and Tony Karayianni
aka Tori Carrington

TORI CARRINGTON
Reckless

HARLEQUIN®

TORONTO • NEW YORK • LONDON
AMSTERDAM • PARIS • SYDNEY • HAMBURG
STOCKHOLM • ATHENS • TOKYO • MILAN • MADRID
PRAGUE • WARSAW • BUDAPEST • AUCKLAND

ISBN-13: 978-0-373-79437-9
ISBN-10: 0-373-79437-1

RECKLESS

Copyright © 2008 by Lori and Tony Karayianni.

www.eHarlequin.com

Printed in U.S.A.

ABOUT THE AUTHOR

Multi-award-winning, bestselling husband-and-wife duo Lori and Tony Karayianni are the power behind the pen name Tori Carrington. Their more than thirty-five titles include numerous Harlequin Blaze miniseries, as well as the ongoing Sofie Metropolis comedic mystery series with another publisher. Visit www.toricarrington.net and www.sofiemetro.com and www.myspace.com/toricarrington for more information on the couple and their titles.

We dedicate this book to all our MySpace and Facebook friends. You guys rock!

And, as always, to our editor Brenda Chin, who has a knack for seeing the forest despite the trees.

1

HOT BREATH created a steamy dampness on her neck, challenging the summer heat for dominance… Her nipples awakened to tingling life under the attention of his roaming hands… She tightened her thighs, trapping his hips, a moan building in her throat…

Heidi Joblowski arched her back against the cool sheets and slid her hands down to cup Jesse's bottom, holding him close.

Oh, yes…

He instantly stiffened against her, his body quaking.

Oh, no.

Not again. Not yet.

Heidi bit her bottom lip, praying that this wasn't it. That Jesse wasn't finished.

He collapsed against her.

The moan turned into a groan.

"Mmm," he hummed, kissing her neck several times and then kissing her mouth. "That was good. You were good."

Apparently she was too good. He'd reached climax before she was even halfway up the ladder, leaving her hanging from the rungs with no hope of his helping her over. Because she knew that no matter what she said, what she did, he was done.

And she wasn't even close.

"What?" he said when she kissed him back with moderate enthusiasm. "Oh, no. Did I do it again?"

Heidi took a deep breath, trying to unwind her coiled muscles. "When I said 'quickie,' I didn't mean it in a literal sense. I meant 'no foreplay necessary.' But an orgasm would have been nice."

He chuckled into her hair. "I'm sorry, Heidi."

She stretched her neck, figuring she could see to herself in the shower. After all, it was three o'clock on a busy Saturday afternoon in June and she certainly hadn't expected more. Had hoped for more, especially since they'd spoken several times lately about Jesse's habit of not waiting for her before diving over the orgasmic edge.

Of course, all it usually took for Jesse was a gentle blow in his ear and a squeeze of her thighs and he was a goner.

Therein lay the problem.

"It's the place, I think," he said, smoothing her hair back from her face. "It's strange having sex in Professor Tanner's place."

"It's not his place, it's mine. At least for the summer while I'm renting it from him."

Well, she was actually house-sitting, as well. Watering Tanner's plants, taking care of his garden, forwarding his mail to him while he was in Belgium for the next couple of months. A perfect set-up, really. She got the type of privacy with Jesse that she wanted and that they couldn't have at the apartment he shared with two friends, and all she had to do was take care of the house as if it were her own. Perfect.

Only it wasn't working as well as she'd hoped.

Jesse turned on his dazzling megawatt grin. "Do you want to try again?"

Heidi quickly reached for another condom on the nightstand.

A knock at the front door thwarted her intentions.

Jesse kissed her. "I'll make it up to you, Hi. I promise."

She languidly snaked her arms around his neck and tunneled her fingers into his thick, dark hair. "At this rate, you'll owe me well into the next century," she whispered.

His chuckle made her smile. "So be it." He kissed her deeply again before pushing off to jump into his jeans sans underwear. "I can come up with worse debts."

So could she.

Heidi propped herself up on her elbows, watching Jesse Gilbred's fine male form as he got dressed. His tousled hair dipped low over his brow. His slender, whipcord-taut muscles moved and rippled with his actions. His green eyes twinkled at her mischievously.

It was a sight of which she'd never tire. She'd met Jesse when they'd been little more than kids in high school and had remained smitten with him ever since. He'd been the captain of the football team, she'd been the quiet, studious girl from the wrong side of the tracks. Even when he'd left Fantasy, Michigan, to attend college in the east, they'd maintained a long-distance relationship, with Jesse returning at least one weekend a month to see her. It had been a long two years, but when he'd graduated and come home for good to work in a managerial capacity at his father's construction company, she'd been there for him, just as she had for the past eight years.

He had been her first. And she intended that he be

her last. He was the one she'd built all of her plans around. Well, all but the little detail they encountered every now and again, as they had just now. But they could definitely work on that.

He left the room and Heidi pulled a pillow over her head and gave a muffled moan.

"Hey, how's it hanging, man?" she heard Jesse's voice as he greeted their visitor.

She shifted the pillow to peek at the bedroom door he'd left wide open.

Jesse's best friend entered her line of vision, all blond hair and dark tan. He stared at her, apparently as startled as she was at being caught in this situation.

"Jesse!" she called, yanking the sheet up to her chin and then catapulting off the bed so she could close the door.

Heidi leaned against the wood for long moments, listening to Jesse's laugh and Kyle's awkward apologies.

So much for seeing to her own needs. Whatever lingering desire she felt had been chased away by another man's scorching gaze.

She made out Jesse's words through the wood, "No need to apologize. If a guy can't trust his best friend, who can he trust?"

Heidi gave an eye roll and dropped the sheet, stepping over it on her way to the connecting bath.

NAKED as the day she was born.

The ridiculous saying came to Kyle Trapper's mind as he raked his hand through his hair, staring at his friend as if he'd lost a baseball or two on the way to the game.

Kyle had yet to move from where he stood in the middle of the small, well-appointed living room. His gaze wandered back toward the closed bedroom door of its own volition, as if hoping to catch another forbidden glimpse of Heidi's decadent white flesh. He didn't care which part. Whether it was her pert, rose-kissed breasts, her flat, toned stomach, or the trimmed triangle of hair that seemed to point toward the V of her thighs like an erotic arrow.

His friend sat on an armchair pulling on socks and athletic shoes, oblivious to his thoughts. And it was a good thing. If their roles had been reversed, he'd have punched his friend.

"Hell, Jesse, do you let everyone see your girl-friend naked?"

Jesse got up and smacked him on the back. "Only my closest friends."

Kyle was not amused.

"What's your problem? You'd think you'd never seen a woman without her clothes on."

"Never that woman."

Never Jesse's girl.

Jesse grabbed a T-shirt that was hanging on the back of the chair. "How'd you know I was here, anyway?"

Kyle hadn't known. In fact, he hadn't come here for his friend at all. He'd come to talk to Heidi.

He cleared his throat. "Where else would you be?"

His response must have come out gruffer than he'd intended because Jesse paused. "Hey, you never have told me what your problem is with Heidi, but she's one of the most open women I've ever met." He shrugged as he pulled the shirt over his head. "She won't care that you've seen her naked."

"Right. That's why she turned ten shades of red and

slammed the door." Kyle rubbed the back of his neck. "And why do you think I have a problem with her?"

Jesse pulled the T-shirt down, revealing the name of a local tavern. "She thinks you don't like her."

That surprised him. At the same time it was cause for relief. If either Jesse or Heidi had a clue about how he really felt…well, he didn't think he'd be standing in her rental house right now, about to leave with her boyfriend to play softball.

In fact, he'd probably be run out of the small town on a rail, back to a life that had never held much for him by way of a future.

If you had asked him seven years ago where he'd be now, he would never have guessed south-east Michigan, working as an architect. But that would have been before Jesse was assigned as his roommate at Boston University and his life had changed forever…for the better. So much so that he hadn't hesitated when his friend had invited him to come to Fantasy eight months ago and put his architectural talents to good use by working in cooperation with Gilbred Builders. So he'd shut the doors to his own start-up company in Boston and moved to the Midwest.

He'd like to say it had been smooth sailing ever since. But he wasn't much into lying, particularly to himself. Until he'd moved to Fantasy, he'd only spoken to Heidi when she called and Jesse wasn't home—calls he'd enjoyed more than he should have. What he hadn't anticipated was that coming to Fantasy would amplify his lust for a woman he could never have.

If he'd needed a reminder, he'd just gotten it by way

of his uncomfortable physical reaction to a mere glimpse of her full-frontal nudity.

And what of his strategy to combat his unwanted emotions by asking her to help him plan a surprise birthday party for Jesse? The idea being that the more time he forced himself to spend around her, the better he'd be able to battle against his attraction to her? Was he kidding himself by thinking that familiarity would erase whatever mysterious factors drew him to her?

But after eight months of careful avoidance and awkward silences whenever their paths crossed, and nights filled with countless cold showers, Kyle knew he had to do something to defuse a situation that was only getting worse instead of better.

"Anyway, we all know you're gay," Jesse said, lightly hitting him in the arm.

"What?"

"You heard me. I haven't seen you date a single woman since you've come to Fantasy. Back in Boston you were with a girl nearly every night of the week. I figured you'd switched sides and were batting lefty."

Now that was a new one. But, hey, so long as it kept his best friend from learning the truth, let him think what he would.

"I'm joking, man."

Kyle stared at him, realizing that Jesse had expected something else from him. A denial maybe. Or perhaps a mock physical assault.

He made like he was going to slug him.

Jesse laughed and good-naturedly dodged the hit as he grabbed his ball cap. "Come on. We can get in some practice on the field before anyone else gets there."

Jesse opened the front door and walked out. Kyle stood staring at the closed bedroom door for a long moment, feeling as if he owed Heidi an apology. He heard the spray of the shower and swallowed thickly, the sound of the water combining with the memory of her sleekly naked body to create an image he really didn't need.

The blare of a truck horn sounded from the driveway.

Kyle gave the door one last glance and then reluctantly turned away. If he knew what was best for him, he'd keep on going until he was back in Boston and well away from a temptation that had the potential to destroy all the good he'd finally found in life.

THE TOWN PUB was a popular gathering place all year round, but in the summer, doubly so. Heidi shouted her order to the bartender over the cacophony of voices. Most of the patrons had come from the baseball complex on the edge of town, like her. She peeled off the money to pay for the beer and then juggled the five bottles as she made her way back to the table. Unsurprisingly, she found that Jesse had left his chair and was playing darts with Kyle. He took two beers from her as she passed.

"Thanks, babe."

He kissed her cheek but his focus was on the target some ten feet away. She put the remaining beers on the table and sat down next to her friend Nina Leonard.

Actually, Nina was more than a friend. She was Heidi's boss at BMC, the bookstore/music center/café where she'd been working for the past year while she finished her degree at U of M. And Nina was partners in more ways than one with the man sitting on the other side of her, Kevin Weber. The two were due to marry in a couple of months, surprising almost everyone with their rapid courtship. To this day, half the town's population watched Nina's stomach, convinced she must be pregnant.

Heidi knew they were getting married because they were in love.

"When are you going to ask Jesse to stop calling you a pig's name?" Nina asked, quirking a brow at her.

Heidi made a face. "He doesn't mean it that way."

Nina looked at Kevin. He pretended he didn't have a clue what they were talking about.

"Oh, stop it," Heidi said with a laugh.

"Hey, you're the one who pitched a fit when Jesse proposed at the wrong time," Nina reminded her.

Heidi cringed and leaned her forehead against her open palm. "Oh, God, I knew I shouldn't have told you about that."

"If not me, then who?" Nina leaned in closer. "If I wasn't already engaged to Kevin, I'd give Jesse's friend Kyle another look or two."

Heidi gaped at her.

"What? I can look." Nina waggled her fingers. "It's the touching I can't do."

Kevin gave his fiancée a long stare and then slid from the booth, gravitating toward the men playing darts and away from the women talking men.

Heidi watched him go, wondering not for the first time what had gone down at BMC several months ago and why the third partner in the business, Patrick Gauge, had disappeared without explanation. For as long as

Heidi had been at the store, she'd believed Nina, Kevin and Gauge were the closest of friends.

Then Gauge had left. And Nina and Kevin had become engaged.

While she wasn't one for gossip—well, not much, anyway—Heidi hadn't been able to ignore the rumors surrounding her bosses. While there were several versions of the story, all of them centered around one theme: a steamy love triangle.

Was it true? Heidi didn't know and wouldn't allow herself to ask. But she'd be lying if she said that questioning glances like the one Kevin had just given Nina after her innocent remarks about Kyle didn't make her wonder every now and again.

And just the other day, after a run-in with the new manager of BMC's music department, which Gauge had once overseen, she'd absently said to Nina, "I miss Gauge."

Her friend had gotten a faraway look and whispered, "Me, too."

Now, Nina took a deep pull from her beer bottle. "Tell me again why you refused the ring."

"Would you stop already?" Heidi laughed.

"Okay. Then tell me about this idea of how you want your life to unfold."

"It's a plan."

"Excuse me. Plan." Nina gave her a sidelong glance. "And Jesse's proposal before the appointed time sent everything into a tailspin."

Heidi sighed. "I know. It sounds stupid, doesn't it? I mean, most women would be thrilled to be proposed to at all. Much less by a hot guy like Jesse."

"Yes, well, you're not most women. You and Jesse have been a couple for, like, forever. And you've always seen yourself getting engaged…when?"

"You know when." Heidi held the cold bottle against the side of her face to cool her heated skin. "When I get my MBA. What's so wrong with that?"

"Which is when?"

"Since I'm taking summer classes now, I'm hoping for early next year."

"So, let me get this straight. When did Jesse propose?"

"Last week."

"So he popped the question a whole six months before your idea of when you thought he should propose and you turned him down?"

Heidi was affronted. "I didn't turn him down. I just told him to ask me next year."

Nina counted off on her fingers. "First there's the proposal after you've graduated. Preferably on the night you accept your diploma. Then there's a one-year-to-the-date wedding at St. Pat's. And nine months after that, your first child…" Nina tucked her short, neat, blond hair behind her ear. "You know, you really can't plan stuff like that, Heidi."

"Why not?"

Nina shrugged and sipped her beer. "I know that everything's gone according to plan so far. And that there's no reason to think it won't now…" Her words trailed off and she got that faraway look again.

"But?" Heidi asked quietly, feeling oddly sober.

Nina blinked and smiled softly. "But sometimes life doesn't turn out the way you expect it to."

"Talking about me again?"

Heidi looked up into Jesse's handsome face, returning his kiss with gusto. "Always."

He pulled up a chair next to her while Kyle did the same on the opposite side of the table. Heidi met his gaze briefly and felt heat suffuse her from the top of her head down to the tip of her toes. She'd avoided looking directly at him since their little…encounter earlier at the house. It wasn't every day someone who wasn't her boyfriend saw her naked.

She wasn't sure what she expected to see. An apology, maybe? Or perhaps even a knowing smirk?

Instead Kyle wore an expression she couldn't quite define. And for the span of a millisecond she felt the type of electricity she'd experienced only one other time in her life: the day she'd met Jesse.

She blinked, shocked to find herself suddenly breathless.

"So what did you guys think of the game?" Jesse asked, flexing his right biceps. "Did we rock or what?"

Everyone shouted a response either pro or con as Heidi quickly looked away from Kyle.

She was relieved that when she glanced back, Kyle was no longer looking at her but at the waitress putting a fresh bowl of peanuts on the table.

"Pity the man who has to sing his own praises," he said.

"And praise the man who doesn't have to," Kevin agreed.

The table erupted into laughter.

Heidi picked up her beer bottle and drained half the contents, feeling strangely as though she'd just grabbed a live wire.

And she hadn't a clue how to let go…

2

KEEP THINGS LIGHT. Keep things safe.

Kyle repeated the words in his mind three days later as he climbed out of his car in the parking lot of BMC, the bookstore/music center/café where Heidi worked. He shaded his eyes, spotting Heidi's old Sunfire convertible parked a couple of rows up. Good, she was working. That meant that he could talk to her in the safe environment of her workplace, *safe* being a relative term.

At any rate, he was sure there would be little risk of seeing her naked here. It was hard enough being with her and Jesse in public without imagining her sans clothes.

Which made what he was about to ask doubly difficult.

"Oh, for God's sake, she's just a woman. More than that, she's your best friend's girl. Get over it."

But no matter how stridently he censured himself, he knew that the attraction he felt for Heidi far surpassed coveting his buddy's girlfriend. From the moment he'd ridden into Fantasy and had finally met Heidi, he'd known he was in trouble.

And he had done everything in his power to fight the unwanted feelings.

"Kyle?"

He pulled his gaze from Heidi's car to find himself

looking at Heidi herself. She was wearing her work apron, the white fabric snug against her slender frame. It was as if she'd emerged from his thoughts, looking somehow out of place in the parking lot.

He realized he hadn't said anything yet and managed a simple, "Hey."

She walked in his direction. "What are you doing here?"

He squinted at her.

"Trying to expand your horizons by buying a book?"

He stuffed his hands into the pockets of his slacks. He'd taken off his suit jacket and rolled up the sleeves of his white shirt, but still wore his tie. "Actually, I heard the clam chowder was pretty good here."

Her smile eclipsed the sun. "The best, considering I'm the one who makes it."

"You going somewhere?"

She glanced over her shoulder and then at her watch. "Yeah. I thought I'd get a few errands out of the way during my break."

"I was hoping we could talk."

Now that hadn't come out quite the way he'd wanted. It almost sounded like what he had to say was personal. While it was, it wasn't the kind of "personal" that should have inspired the wary look on her beautiful face.

She checked her watch again. "I'm sorry, but I really don't have the time. I only have fifteen minutes before I have to be back at work."

Kyle grimaced. Probably he should have just gone in and ordered and waited for her to come back. Now if he did that, she'd likely avoid him at all costs.

Hell.

"It's not what you might be thinking," he said.

"I'm not thinking anything," she said, beginning to walk away. "Why would I be thinking anything?" She shrugged. "You know, aside from you going out of your way to be rude to me ever since you came to town eight months ago."

"Pardon?"

She planted her hands on her hips. "You heard me. I mean, come on, Kyle, did you think I wouldn't notice that you don't like me very much? I don't know why that is…and I don't want to know. So why don't we just continue on the way we have been. You know, with chilly cordiality?"

Chilly cordiality? Now that was a description.

Unending cold showers would be more his choice of wording.

He looked her over. She really didn't have a clue, did she? Despite the other night at the bar when he was afraid he'd revealed more than he'd ever intended to, she thought he didn't like her.

Which should have suited him just fine.

But suddenly it didn't.

"I've really got to go…"

She turned to walk away. And without realizing he was going to do it, he grasped her wrist to prevent her from leaving.

"We really need to talk, Heidi."

HEAT, sure and swift, swept over Heidi's skin from the casual contact. A heat she didn't want to acknowledge. There was only one thing worse than the possibility of being attracted to her boyfriend's best friend: knowing that he didn't return the sentiment. In fact, she was convinced that not only was Kyle not interested in her sexually, he wasn't interested in befriending her either, no matter how hard Jesse tried to push them together.

"I don't know what we could possibly have to talk about," she told him now.

Liar. She could start by telling him how something had changed in her feelings toward him the other night. Something elemental. Something confusing. Something frightening.

Nina had told her that plans often didn't turn out exactly the way you wanted them to. That wasn't Heidi's experience. At least not in recent years. And she didn't even want to consider that her well-laid plans would go anywhere but where they should. She'd been raised in an environment where simple things like cooking dinner and regularly paying the electric bill hadn't been planned, so she'd taken it upon herself to impose order on her own life. As soon as she was old enough, she'd gotten herself up and to the bus stop on time, changing from an often-tardy student to one with no late slips. She'd gone grocery shopping with her mother, and while Alice Joblowski had lingered in the book section leafing through the latest titles, Heidi had consulted a list she'd made of ingredients for meals for the next two weeks, because you never knew when her mother would think to go to the supermarket next.

She liked order in her life.

And her reaction to Kyle's skin against hers now was nothing if not disordered.

She slipped her wrist out of his grip.

"Look," he said, shoving his hand back into his pocket, seeming as irritated as she was. "I know you and I…well, we haven't really gotten on well since I moved here. But Jesse would like to change that. And, frankly, so would I."

Heidi frowned. "I'm okay with the way things are."

He looked at her closely. Perhaps a little too closely.

"What is it that you want to talk about, Kyle?" She made a point of checking her watch again. At this rate, she'd be late returning from break. And she hadn't finished one of the three errands she'd wanted to run.

"I want you to help me plan a surprise birthday party for Jesse."

"A SURPRISE birthday party?" Nina repeated sometime later, after Heidi had returned to work.

The two women were in the café's kitchen, Nina sitting on the prep table snacking on oyster crackers while Heidi put all her energy into kneading a fresh batch of sweet dough.

Usually, this was one of her favorite times of day. When the morning baking and the lunch rush were over and she could enjoy the afterglow of a job well done and kvetch or gossip with Nina while she tried out a new recipe.

Sometimes it was difficult to remember that Nina Leonard was her boss. Nina certainly never put on any airs, and she always treated Heidi like a coworker rather than an employee. Ideas were exchanged, schedules switched. And there wasn't a thing Heidi couldn't tell Nina.

Her cheeks felt as if they were on fire…along with her pants. What was the saying? Liar, liar, pants on fire?

There was one thing she wouldn't dare tell Nina. And that was anything having to do with her recent sexual awareness of Kyle. To do so would be the ultimate in reckless, and even worse, it would be taking that awareness beyond a real fear to a very real reality.

"So what did you tell him?" Nina popped another cracker into her mouth.

Heidi slowed her kneading. "What was I supposed to tell him?"

"That you had to check your schedule?"

She pinched off a bit of dough and threw it at Nina. "I told him yes, of course."

Kyle had offered a convincing case. Said he wasn't used to organizing parties but wanted to do this one thing for his best friend to make a dent in the debt he owed Jesse for helping him out on so many occasions.

"What do you know about this guy?" Nina asked.

Heidi shrugged. "That he and Jesse met at college. That they roomed together for two years. He's an architect and works a lot in cooperation with Jesse's family's company…"

"What about personally?"

"Like how?"

"Like does he have a girlfriend?"

"Not that I can tell. Jesse and I haven't really discussed it."

Nina pushed off the counter and threw away the dough stuck to her shirt. "I'd be careful there."

Heidi's kneading came to a full stop. "How do you mean?"

"I don't know. You could say that I've had a little experience being…friends with two hot men."

Heidi remembered the rumors and was tempted to ask about them. But the telephone rang, like some sort of physical warning that she should just leave well enough alone. She was mildly surprised that Nina didn't seem to hear it. Someone must have picked it up out front.

"Anyway," Nina said, checking the progress of another bowl of dough that was rising on top of the warm stove. "I just think it's important for you to be careful."

"I'm not following you."

"You know, you might not want to be…alone with Kyle during any of the planning meetings…stuff like that."

Heidi laughed. "Don't be ridiculous. Jesse and I have been a couple for eight years."

"Just the same…"

Janice, the front-counter girl, opened the door a crack. "Heidi, it's for you."

Her throat suddenly went dry. Nina's gaze sharpened on her.

"I'll finish up," her friend said. "You go talk to whoever it is."

Heidi wiped the dough from her fingers and then quickly washed her hands before picking up the phone in the corner.

"Heidi?"

Her shoulders instantly relaxed and she made a point of saying directly to Nina, who was still watching her, "Hi, Mom."

Then she turned away, not about to admit that she, too, had been half afraid that the call was from Kyle.

She groaned inwardly. However was she going to plan a party with the man if she couldn't deal with the thought of talking to him on the phone?

She didn't know. But she knew that, for Jesse's sake, she was going to have to find a way.

3

HEIDI COULDN'T IMAGINE what her mother wanted her for. It wasn't like Alice to be cagey. But all she'd said on the phone was that she needed to see Heidi and could she please come over to the house when she had the chance?

Heidi put the last of the dough in the fridge and then leaned against the kitchen island and sighed. It was after nine and it had been a long day. But since she wanted tomorrow off for a catering job, she'd needed to put in the hours. She was lucky that Nina and Kevin allowed her to work around her class schedule and whatever else came up. Definitely different from any other employer she'd worked for. And if she wanted to use the kitchen after hours to prepare for any catering gigs that she'd put together, that was all right, too.

Of course, her long day had left her no time to stop by her mother's. Which was just as well, because after the day she'd had, she wasn't sure she was up for any surprises. At least not any more surprises. She had her hands full trying to figure out what she was going to do about Kyle. More specifically, she had to get a handle on her sudden, runaway attraction to him.

Jesse was busy tonight with softball practice and

would no doubt be at the pub with the rest of the gang right about now. She'd spoken to him earlier and bowed out of his invitation to meet him there when she finished. She was tired and, okay, more than a little distracted. She didn't think it was a good idea that she be anywhere near Kyle until she figured out what was going on between them.

Or rather, what was going on with her. Because if there was one thing she was relatively sure of, it was that Kyle Trapper wasn't interested in her. Not one iota. He'd made that abundantly clear with his constant frowns in her presence, and he'd gone out of his way not to interact with her in any capacity.

Until now.

Heidi untied her apron and lifted it over her head, hanging it next to the door before going out into the café. The place was quiet. Nina had left some time ago and asked her to close up shop. She switched off all the lights save the one over the display counter which was always kept lit, and walked toward the music center. It was dark as well except for a couple of back-lights in the public area. The same applied to the book-store division, which was set up to look like a comfortable living room-library combination in a large, century-old house. Although the fireplace was empty of logs, the explosion of flowering plants in the hearth still made it the center of attention, and the overstuffed sofas and chairs invited road-weary shoppers to sit down for a moment and crack open one of the books in carefully arranged stacks on the nearby coffee and end tables.

The utter quiet brought Heidi a brief sense of relief, a

feeling of control that she liked. There were no customers to wait on, no bosses to answer to. Her time was her own.

And she really should be getting home to catch up on her course work.

She checked to make sure the back door was locked, then headed toward the front, clutching her purse to her side. She turned the key to let herself out, and nearly fell backward when someone appeared on the other side of the glass.

It would have been bad enough had it been a stranger. What made it worse was that it was Kyle.

HE'D FRIGHTENED her.

Kyle held open the door, prepared to steady Heidi. He'd been hoping to catch her as she was leaving the store, but he hadn't planned to scare her.

"I'm sorry. I startled you."

"No, no. That's okay," she said quickly, her color high, her breathing uneven. She easily stepped out of touching range.

Damn, but she looked good. Her hair was a dark cloud around her pretty face, her eyes but shadows in the dim light. It had only been a few hours since he'd last seen her, and she'd looked good then. But that had been in the plain light of day. Now that it was night…

"What are you doing here, Kyle?"

Now that was a question.

"When you told me you'd consider my request, we didn't name a time when you'd give me your answer." Kyle's gaze dropped to the pulse at the base of her slender throat. "Since Jesse's birthday's in less than two weeks…I figured that if you don't want to help, I need to know now."

Her frown made her prettier, if that were possible. She looked around the parking lot, where few cars remained. He hadn't parked there.

He didn't think it was a good idea for them to be seen spending time together without a valid reason.

"I'm around back," he said.

She looked at him.

"So have you thought about it?"

"Yes." She dropped her gaze.

"And?"

"And I'm not sure if it's such a good idea."

"The party?"

"Our working together to arrange it."

Kyle raised his brows.

Okay, he'd be lying if he said he hadn't picked up on the spark of attraction that had ignited between them, turning what had been his one-sided lusting into a reciprocal need.

Probably it wasn't a good idea to encourage that, considering she was his best friend's girl. But he'd been mentally planning Jesse's twenty-fifth birthday party for months now. And he was determined to make it a reality.

"We're adults, aren't we?" he asked.

"What?"

"We're both capable of putting aside personal differences so that we can work together."

She gestured with her hand. "Sure."

She didn't look too sure.

Causing Kyle to look more closely at her.

Footsteps sounded on the sidewalk and then the jingling of keys. "Good night, Heidi," a middle-aged man from the next-door business called as he locked up.

"Yes…good night, Mr. Bannon. See you tomorrow morning."

Bannon glanced at Kyle and nodded once.

He returned the gesture. Even though he'd been in Fantasy for a relatively short time, he still hadn't gotten used to how small a town it was. Everybody seemed to know everybody else's business.

"Um, I think we should go inside," Heidi whispered, although there was no longer anyone around to hear her.

Kyle didn't argue as she opened the door and ducked inside. He followed, waiting for her to lock the doors before leading the way through the bookstore, then the music center until finally they were in the café where she worked.

She stopped in the middle of the room, the display case backlighting her sexy form. She appeared about ready to jump out of her skin as she took in the large window overlooking the walk and the parking lot beyond.

"The kitchen." She gestured over her shoulder. "I think it's better if we go in there."

Moments later, Kyle stood across a large, stainless-steel island from Heidi, wondering why she was acting as if he posed some sort of threat to her. He didn't look threatening, did he? He slid his hands in his pockets and grimaced. "This is where you work then? In the kitchen?"

Stupid question. He knew she was a certified chef. That she had a busy catering business and that as soon as she obtained her MBA she planned to apply for a loan to expand the company to include employees and her own store front.

"Yes," she said simply.

The place was quieter than he'd expected. Not that he'd thought about it much, but it struck him as odd that beyond the hum of the refrigerator, there was no other sound.

"So…" they said at the same time.

A smile.

Kyle chuckled.

"This is awkward, isn't it?" Heidi crossed her arms under her breasts, drawing his attention to the soft mounds under her clingy black T-shirt. Was it him, or had she just shivered?

She followed his gaze and immediately uncrossed her arms.

"I guess we should start with the basics," she said. She felt around her hips as if looking for something. "I'm not wearing my apron." It was hanging near the door and she went over and took out a hand-sized spiral notepad from the pocket. She opened it, put it down on the counter and clicked her pen.

Kyle realized she'd spoken but he hadn't heard what she'd said. "Pardon me?"

"What have you done so far?" she repeated. "Have you decided on a venue? Your house? Or maybe his parents' place?"

"I was hoping you could help me with that."

She wrote something down. "Guests? Who do you want to invite?"

An hour later, they'd pretty much worked out the major details of the party.

Kyle couldn't help feeling that despite how tired she looked, Heidi appeared to want to get this over with in one meeting. Probably so she wouldn't have to see him again. The rest could easily be taken care of over the phone.

It didn't sit well with him that she was uncomfortable in his presence. Was it because he'd seen her naked the other day? Or were her reasons a secret? A mystery even to herself?

Whatever the cause, he found himself wanting to put her at ease.

"Heidi…?"

"Hmm?" She was putting her notepad back into her apron pocket, and she turned quickly, ending up almost nose to nose with him. There was little maneuvering room, with the wall at her back.

"Oh!"

Kyle's throat suddenly felt tight as he watched her pink tongue flick along her bottom lip.

He leisurely took his fill of her up this close. He hadn't noticed the light spattering of freckles across the bridge of her nose, or the specks of deep green in her warm brown eyes. And she smelled of…was that gardenia?

"Thank you," he said quietly.

"For what?" Her voice was a mere whisper as she returned the same attention to him that he was giving her.

Kyle smiled. "For going in on this with me."

Her gaze darted around the room. "Sure, no problem."

"Are you certain? Because I'm getting the impression that there is a problem."

"Like what?"

He shrugged, his palms itching with the desire to reach out and touch her. "That's what I'm wondering. You don't seem to want to be in a room alone with me for any stretch." God, but she smelled good. His voice lowered. "Why is that?"

He heard the catch in her breathing. "Don't be silly. You're Jesse's best friend."

And she was Jesse's girl.

The thought should have been enough to chase Kyle away from the woman in front of him. Should have been enough to remind him that not only was she taken, but she had Jesse's name stamped all over her. While they weren't engaged, they were *practically* engaged. The two had been a couple for almost a decade.

"And any friend of Jesse's is a friend of yours?" he finished for her.

She nodded, her pupils nearly eclipsing the rich color of her eyes as she stared at him unblinkingly.

And maybe that's what she needed to do. What he needed to do. Give a good blink to break whatever spell being this close to each other was casting over them.

He closed his eyes and took a deep breath.

Then opened them to find that he should probably have shared his thoughts with her. Because Heidi was doing what he had hoped to prevent. She was leaning in to kiss him.

4

OH, MY GOD…

Heidi wasn't entirely sure what she was doing. It looked like she was kissing Kyle. But that was impossible. There was no way she would ever kiss her boyfriend's best friend.

She heard a small sound and realized that not only was she kissing Kyle, she was doing so wholeheartedly—and enjoying it.

Enjoying it? Hell, she was afraid she might spontaneously combust from the simple contact of her mouth against his.

She abruptly broke off the kiss, only to find Kyle's hands on either side of her face, allowing her no quarter.

Heidi swallowed thickly, incapable of movement, incapable of doing anything more than stare at him, wondering what he made of her actions…and, more, wondering how he might respond to her.

In that one moment, she knew that she'd risked everything she'd worked so hard for. Jeopardized every last plan, every last intention.

And when Kyle leaned in to kiss her again, she knew that she'd do it all over again in a heartbeat.

She wasn't sure what it was about this one man,

what made her yearn for him in a way she was unable to resist. Perhaps it was the way she saw herself through his eyes: sexy, desirable, wanted. Or maybe it was her need of an unnameable something in him that compelled her to reach out. Something fundamental that transcended simple sexual need, consequences be damned.

Where before their kiss had been tentative, testing, now it was hungry and demanding. As if they both understood that they'd already thrown caution to the wind, risked so much, so why not just go the whole way?

Oh, yes. Why not?

Heidi couldn't seem to kiss Kyle enough…touch him enough. She sought and licked and stroked from his crisp, thick hair to the back waist of his slacks. He pressed her against the wall, his mouth demanding as he grasped her hands and pulled them above her head, trapping them against the cool drywall even as he ground his hips into hers. Heidi moaned, the pressure he applied on the outside spreading to her inside, swirling and growing as she hooked her foot around his calf, drawing him closer still.

She struggled to regain control of her hands and he released her, moving her instead toward the preparation island. If she'd thought the wall was cool, she shivered when he hoisted her up to sit on the stainless steel, coaxing her knees apart with his hips and then filling the void with his body. Heidi tunneled her fingers into his hair, hauling him in for another kiss, a deeper kiss, her breathing coming in quick gasps. She reached for his shirt buttons and then roughly pulled the shirt up, separating herself from him briefly until the white cotton lay in a pile in the corner. He did the same with her shirt and her bra, leaving her bare to his attentions. The image of him running his tongue along her engorged nipples was almost too much to endure.

She'd never been intimate with any man except Jesse. Merely watching Kyle take liberties with her, claim her with a passionate certainty, nearly brought her to the brink.

"I have no fantasies," she'd told Nina not too long ago.

Her friend had stared at her as if she were nuts.

But Heidi had never had any need for fantasies. Not when reality provided everything she wanted.

As she helped Kyle peel her slacks off, she wondered if perhaps she should have found something to fantasize about. Because maybe if she had, she wouldn't have allowed definite fantasy material to seep into her reality.

Kyle's fingers probed her throbbing flesh. She threw her head back and groaned, her hands flat against the counter, her hips bucking involuntarily.

How long had it been since she'd experienced this insane heat? This chaotic need? To be sure, up until recently, Jesse and her sex life had been satisfying.

Oh, but not this hot.

Two years? Five years?

The thoughts muddled in her brain as Kyle fitted a finger into her dripping wetness, rendering her helpless to do anything more than concentrate on him and only him.

Was this what it was like? Playing the field? Inviting intimacy with multiple men?

God, if this was any indication, then she'd lived a very sheltered life, indeed.

The problem was, she was terrified that the incredible heat she was experiencing wasn't the result of exploring new territory with just any man…but only with Kyle.

"No…no…no…" she whispered, biting hard on her bottom lip even as she hastily undid the button on his fly and reached in to cup his silken length.

"Yes…yes…yes," she countered.

If Kyle was tuned into her internal dilemma, he wasn't letting on. Every bit of flesh he uncovered seemed to fascinate him endlessly, and his hands and mouth would follow his gaze, leaving no inch unexplored.

Heidi was in awe of his absorption. As was her body. She ached in a way that left her breathless, her heart racing uncontrollably.

Then came the moment when he would cross that last line, breach the last barrier.

Sheathed with a condom, he grasped her hips and stared into her eyes.

Heidi's chest felt tight, her every cell shimmering with desire at this unexpected act of courtesy.

She licked her lips repeatedly and then scooted even closer to the edge of the counter.

"Please," she said in response to his unspoken question.

He groaned, only too happy to oblige.

HEAVEN, hell and grandma's devil's food cake all rolled up into one hot package.

That's how Kyle would have described finally being able to touch Heidi. But no one was asking, including himself. Because to bring any sort of gravity into the moment would completely negate the need for the question itself.

Oh, he knew that the last thing he should be doing

was baring the true way he felt about Heidi, especially to Heidi herself. But, damn it, the instant her soft lips had met his, he'd been incapable of doing any differently. He'd lived with his desire for her for so long that he couldn't have stopped himself if he tried.

His heart beat unevenly in his chest as he fitted himself against her slick portal. She'd given him the go-ahead. That's all he needed just now. He'd deal with the rest afterward…

Heidi shivered and curved her feet around his hips, bringing her vulva to rest solidly against his pulsing length. He watched, fascinated, as she leaned back against her arms, proudly displaying her full breasts, their pink tips seeming to scream out to him for attention. He bent to take one stiff nipple into his mouth, rolling it around like a pebble on his tongue as he entered her in one smooth, long stroke.

Her moan wound around him more tightly than her legs, reaching for something inside of him he hadn't known was there. He slid his hands up over her hips and then under her, providing a pad against the hard surface as he pulled her slightly over the edge of the counter and then entered her again.

Sweet mercy…

She felt better than any woman had a right to.

He told himself that he was reacting so powerfully to her because he'd gone so long without a woman's company. But he'd never been very good at lying, not even to himself.

He grasped the flesh of her bottom more tightly, holding her still as he thrust into her again, the action causing her breasts to jiggle. He gritted his back teeth, staving off climax. No. He'd waited too damn long for this for it to be over so quickly.

Kyle paced himself, slowing his strokes until his balls felt as though they might explode. Yes. That was…

Heidi's back arched and she stretched her neck, letting loose a moan that bespoke her own pleasure. Her muscles contracted around him and she shuddered, reaching her own crisis point.

Just knowing that he was the one who had caused her so much pleasure rendered Kyle helpless to withhold his own climax.

HEIDI HAD HEARD of the morning after. But what did you call this?

Whereas she might now be seeking to cuddle with Jesse, she found herself slowly returning to the kitchen counter, hard and cold beneath her back.

Kyle appeared to be experiencing the same intrusion of reality, for while he lay against her, he was stiff and unmoving. And she guessed it wasn't simply because he'd just come, but because he'd come while inside his best friend's girl.

The instant she formulated the thought, Kyle pulled away from her, turning to put himself back together while she pushed up from the counter and did the same.

Oh, my God. What have I done?

Heidi had pulled on her panties and slacks and was reaching for her bra when the floor bucked under her. She grasped the counter edge for balance and closed her eyes tightly against the images of Kyle kissing her, touching her, making love to her.

She'd spent so much of her life avoiding situations

like this that she had no idea what to do now that she had actually gone through one.

"Heidi?"

Kyle's voice was soft behind her.

She held up a hand. "I'm okay."

By okay, she meant that she wasn't about to pass out. But she was by no means okay in the emotional sense.

"Are you sure?"

She forced herself to stand straight and take a few deep breaths, clutching her bra between her breasts as if the lacy material were enough to protect her against the world.

She nodded. "Yes." She smiled at Kyle shakily without really seeing him. "I'm sure."

She reached for her shirt and finished dressing.

Kyle cleared his throat, looking about as comfortable as she was. Which was not at all.

"Maybe I should get going…"

"Maybe you should go…"

They spoke at the same time.

Heidi averted her gaze, completely incapable of looking him in the eye for fear of what she might see there. It didn't matter if it was the cool regard that she was used to seeing from him, or smoldering need; she didn't think she could handle either just then.

"I'll call you later," he said, moving toward the door.

"No. No, don't. Please." Heidi swallowed thickly, hating the plaintive sound in her voice.

"Heidi…"

"Please. Just go."

He did.

5

HEIDI WASN'T SURE what time it was. If forced to guess, she'd say after midnight. She was fuzzy on just how she'd gotten home, or why she'd ended up sitting on the kitchen floor, beyond that she'd gone to the refrigerator to get something cold to drink after a shower and had instead slid to the floor, holding the door open with her foot so that the cold air hit her hot face. She'd long since allowed the door to close but hadn't been able to summon the energy to get up.

She was thankful that Jesse hadn't popped up, as he sometimes did even when she requested time alone. She didn't know what she would have done if he had. In the state she was in, likely she would have spilled everything the moment she opened the door to him.

And then what?

She rested her head against the shelf of her bent knees and tightly closed her eyes.

God, what had she done?

She hadn't known it was humanly possible to want something so badly that you took it regardless of the consequences, only to find those same consequences hitting you in the face the moment after the deed was done. What had been up was now down, what had been right was now wrong.

And where she had been good she was now bad.

"You're so judgmental, Heidi. If you're not careful you're going to be a bitter old woman by twenty-five."

The words were a familiar refrain from her mother and, lately, her sister.

She'd never paid much attention to them and their opinions because, well, she'd always been in the right. She wasn't the single mother of five children from three different men, only one of whom she'd ever been married to. And now her younger sister appeared to be following in their mother's footsteps, marrying as soon as she found out she was pregnant and then divorcing before the kid was even born.

Melody lived on and off with their mother in the same cramped clapboard house where Heidi had been raised, with little more than two nickels to rub together between them at the end of the week.

"And now I'm one of them."

She snapped open her eyes, the words serving to jerk her out of her state of shock.

Everything had happened so quickly she'd only thought about how her actions would impact her life with Jesse. She hadn't stopped to consider the soul-searching she would have to do to understand her actions.

She'd struggled to be such a good girl all her life, but the struggle hadn't been about defeating temptation. Every child born with the name Joblowski had a soiled reputation from day one, and Heidi was determined hers wouldn't be justified. But even though she'd never shown interest in any of the boys throughout middle school, she'd been called Heidi Ho merely through her relationship with her mother and her younger sister

Melody, who had enthusiastically lost her virginity at thirteen and rushed headlong into womanhood without a care in the world.

It wasn't until high school and meeting Jesse that she'd achieved any kind of identity of her own, separate from her family. And she'd always be grateful to him for that.

She rubbed the heel of her hand against her forehead, trying to loosen the tight knot there.

Gathering her wits about her, she slowly got to her feet. She wasn't sure what she was going to do, but whatever it was, losing Jesse wasn't an option. She loved him. He loved her. And there was no reason not to proceed with their plans.

She moved toward the bedroom, realizing she hadn't turned on any of the lights since she'd arrived home, relying on familiarity to find her way.

But what was familiar in her life now? Certainly not what she'd done at the café.

And what about Kyle?

She stumbled over her own feet.

What agenda might Kyle have after tonight? As Jesse's best friend, would he feel compelled to tell Jesse what had happened?

Kyle would go back to being nothing more than Jesse's good friend, she told herself firmly.

KYLE HAD MANAGED to avoid running into Jesse all morning, but couldn't miss the meeting set before lunch because it was the final review of the Kitchner house. He did, however, arrive late, happy to find that things were already moving ahead without him.

"There he is," Jesse said by way of greeting. "If I didn't know better, I'd say you were avoiding me today."

Kyle knew he meant it as a joke. He only wished that it weren't true.

God, what in the hell had inspired him to sleep with his best friend's girl?

The question had kept him up most of the night and he found himself alternately picking up the phone to call Jesse…and Heidi.

He'd awoken to find he hadn't come any closer to an answer than he'd been the night before.

"Do you have the prints for the kitchen redesign?" Jesse asked.

Kyle unrolled the drawing Jesse was looking for on the worktable set up in the foyer of the thirteen-thousand-square-foot mansion they were building together. Jesse was the head of the construction team, Kyle the head architect.

"As you'll see," Jesse was saying to the owner, pointing at the redesign, "when we reconfigure the scheme the way you want, there isn't room for the in-dustrial-sized double-door refrigerator that you chose. One solution—"

Kyle peered at his friend. The issue he was discussing was two design revisions ago.

Thankfully Jesse seemed to catch himself and grimaced at Kyle before pretending the prints were upside down and turning them right again.

"Why don't you explain it to him, Kyle?" Jesse said, looking at his watch. "There's another appointment I need to make in fifteen minutes."

"Sure." Kyle stepped up, clearing his throat to regain the attention of the five men crowded around the table who were watching Jesse instead of the prints. "As you see here…"

He began explaining the proposed adjustment to the room dimensions and offered up alternatives and cost overruns. As soon as he had everyone's attention, he switched to autopilot and watched as Jesse took off his hard hat and then climbed into his truck cab, looking as distracted as Kyle felt.

Was it possible that he knew what had happened last night? Had his friend stopped by the café? But the door had been locked, and so far as he could tell there was no way to see inside the kitchen from the parking lot.

Jesse's tires kicked up gravel as he left the site.

Kyle frowned and finished up. "If you decide to pursue the changes, completion date will be pushed back at least five days."

"Five days?" the owner said.

Kyle began rolling the print back up and shrugged. "It is what it is. The skeleton has already been built and the team already moved to another site. We'd have to pull them back…" He could recite the words in his sleep because he'd run into similar setbacks in nearly every project he'd worked on. Either the wife decided she wanted an Olympic-sized bathtub instead of the regular whirlpool in the original design, or the husband wanted a larger work area. It always meant delays and cost increases.

His cell phone vibrated in his pocket.

He fished it out and started at the caller ID even as he finished up his spiel. Heidi.

"If you'll excuse me a minute, gentlemen, I have to take this call."

"I THINK Jesse knows."

Heidi nearly dropped the plate of boneless chicken breasts she was planning to turn into croquettes for a barbecue that night. She lowered the plate to the counter then stepped away for fear of doing even more damage in her distracted state.

"What do you mean you think Jesse knows?"

"I'm not sure. Did you say anything to him?"

"Me? I haven't even talked to him yet." Heidi realized she was whispering even though she was alone in the house. She paced into the living room. "How about you?"

"I just saw him at a meeting, but he left quickly—like a man with something on his mind. I think he might be on his way to see you."

"Here? Me?"

Heidi stopped cold in the middle of the living room, no longer whispering but bordering on shouting.

Oh, God. Oh, God. Oh, God.

"Heidi? Are you still there?"

Yes. Unfortunately she was.

She made a choking sound that would have to pass for confirmation as she edged nearer the front window and peered around the sheer curtains, looking for Jesse's truck.

"Actually, I'm surprised he isn't there yet."

"Which site are you at?"

He told her.

"That's only a few minutes away. When did he leave?"

"About ten minutes ago."

She swallowed hard. If he'd been coming here, he surely would have arrived by now.

"He hasn't called?"

"No."

"You've had your phone on?"

"Of course I've had my phone on. I may not like what happened, but I'm not about to hide from it."

Or whatever happened as a result of it.

She'd worked on various explanations all morning while cooking for the Johnson barbecue, where she would be both caterer and guest…along with Jesse and probably Kyle and half of Fantasy, Michigan.

"Are you going to tell him?" Kyle asked quietly.

Heidi bit her bottom lip. "I don't know yet. What about you?"

"I'm kind of playing this by ear."

She heard him curse, cutting off her need to do the same.

Heidi resumed her pacing, staring at the empty driveway every time she headed in that direction.

If Kyle was right, and Jesse planned on coming to the house, she'd have to face him and make her decision about how to handle the situation sooner than she would have liked. But if given a choice between sooner or later, she supposed it was probably better to get everything out in the open now. If only so they could begin the healing process.

"You know, there's always the option of not telling him," Kyle said softly.

Heidi gripped the telephone receiver tightly, vivid images of his hands against her skin, the expression on his face as he'd reached climax sliding easily through her mind.

"I know," she whispered.

She heard another voice on his end and he said, "Look, I've got to go."

"Sure," she said. "Okay."

"Is he there yet?"

Heidi checked through the curtains again. "No. Not yet."

"Okay."

She wanted to ask what he was thinking, but decided she had enough to work out without adding his troubles.

"Heidi?"

"What?"

She realized her voice sounded a little impatient, but, damn it, she figured she was entitled.

So she'd experienced a weak moment. She was only human, right? Surely Kyle should have been the stronger one, stopping what should never have started after she'd kissed him.

"If you need anything…" he said.

"Yeah. I know where to find you."

"Just call."

Oh, trust me, she thought. I will.

6

JESSE HAD never shown up, as Heidi had both feared and hoped would happen. And now that dusk was falling in the nicely decorated backyard of the Johnsons' house, and the townsfolk were gathering for a good old neighborhood barbecue, Heidi had never felt more drained in her life.

It was more than not getting much sleep the night before. Or the fact she'd spent the past nine hours cooking and baking for over a hundred people.

It was her conscience weighing on her like a two-ton truck.

People, both those she knew and strangers, complimented her on the spread, which was impressive by any standards. Homemade baked beans with strips of crisp bacon. Heaping bowls of potato salad, both the creamy and German varieties. Pasta salads, slabs of ribs that only needed to be placed on the grill and slathered with sauce before serving. Chicken croquettes, along with the expected hamburgers and hotdogs, made gourmet by her own seasoning blend and served in homemade cheese-and-onion buns with spicy chili.

Then there was the dessert table…

"Have you seen him yet?"

The sound of Kyle's voice against the back of her neck as she wiped ketchup from the linen tablecloth made her jump.

"Whoa," he said, touching her arm to steady her as she turned to face him. As he looked at her, his expression relaxed and a warm gleam entered his eyes.

Heidi swallowed. "I don't think it's a good idea for you to be standing so close."

"Why?"

"Because normally you wouldn't be caught dead within five feet of me, that's why." Her gaze darted around the diners. "People will get the wrong idea."

"And what idea's that?"

"That we're suddenly a couple."

"And that would be so bad how?"

Heidi opened her mouth then snapped it shut. "Are you serious? Tell me you're not serious."

Laughter caught her attention. Familiar laughter.

She pushed Kyle away and craned her neck to watch Jesse heartily greeting other guests. The setting sun gave his dark hair highlights of spun gold and deepened his tan. She remembered as a teen, seeing him running from the football field for the first time in similar light. Her heart had pitched to her feet and sprung up again straight into the sky. Then he'd grinned at her and she'd dissolved into a puddle at his cleats.

Had that really been so long ago? When was the last time she'd felt that desire to lie down before him, offer herself up as a sort of human sacrifice?

Don't be silly, she ordered herself. She was an adult now. And adults didn't do that.

Her gaze slid to Kyle and her knees weakened.

"There's my girl!" Jesse was in front of her and swept her up into his arms. A habit of his that had become irritating to her lately. And now was no exception.

"Would you stop?" she said, swatting at his wide shoulders. "Put me down."

Heidi cringed, not liking the way she sounded.

Jesse placed her feet on the ground and then gave her a big kiss. She stared at him, wide-eyed.

"You've been avoiding me," he said into her ear. "You know I hate it when you avoid me."

"I've been busy," she said automatically, even though a small voice at the back of her mind told her that he hadn't tried to contact her once all day.

"I can see that. I'm starving. What's on tap?"

KYLE GRIMACED at the scene before him. Jesse and Heidi were every bit the head cheerleader and captain of the football team.

And every bit the couple.

Damn. What had he been thinking by suggesting to Heidi that he wouldn't mind if guests mistook them for being more than friends? She was his best friend's girl, for God's sake. If anything, he should be able to keep that simple thought in his lust-addled brain.

And he'd come to the reluctant conclusion that was what lay at the root of his attraction to Heidi. Lust. Pure and simple. He'd wanted what he couldn't have. She'd been the forbidden fruit and he'd plucked her just because he could.

And now he was paying the price.

He rubbed the back of his neck and forced himself

to turn away from watching Heidi help Jesse fill his plate with food.

Kyle knew hardly anybody here. Which wasn't surprising since he'd only moved to town less than a year ago. A person here and there looked familiar. Probably he'd come across them at the supermarket or gas station. He smiled and nodded his head in greeting, thinking he really should get some food himself, if just to occupy himself with something other than thoughts of Heidi and Jesse and what had transpired last night.

Had it really only been last night? He thought of Einstein's theory of relativity and easily applied it to the situation. It felt as though at least a week had passed since he'd hungrily tasted Heidi's luscious curves— partly because he hadn't sampled nearly as much as he'd have liked. Mostly because, God help him, he could think of little else but savoring her again.

That was all wrong. Wasn't it? Why couldn't he recall the regret he'd heard in her voice earlier? Where was his honor? Shouldn't he be more concerned with whether he was going to explain his behavior to his friend? Or how their activities might affect Heidi's personal sense of integrity?

He caught her gaze, curious to see if he'd find his own thoughts reflected in her eyes.

Kyle cursed under his breath and headed toward the open bar on the other side of the yard. A hand hit him casually in the back. "Going for a brew?" Jesse asked. "Why don't you get one for me while you're at it?"

Kyle glanced over at his friend. "Sure."

Jesse's hand found Kyle's shoulder and he hustled him closer. "I need you to do me a favor, buddy…"

HEIDI WANTED to be anywhere but here. She really needed to think about this Jesse and Kyle issue. Work out what she was going to do and when. She didn't know how long she could pretend that everything was the same without shouting out the truth.

She accepted a plastic cup of draught beer and chugged half of it for courage, nearly spewing it out when she saw Kyle and Jesse huddled together a few feet away. She tried to gauge by their expressions what they were discussing, but came up empty since Jesse seemed to be doing much of the talking, Kyle the listening.

That was good. Wasn't it? At least Kyle wasn't spilling everything to Jesse before she'd had a chance to figure out what she wanted to do.

Kyle's gaze met hers and his eyes darkened. She quickly looked away.

"There's my girl now." Jesse came over and took the half-full cup of beer from her. "Thanks, babe."

Kyle grinned.

Jesse rested his free hand around her waist. "I was just discussing a business matter with Kyle. Seems I'm going to have to travel to Boston to meet with one of our suppliers."

"Oh?" Heidi practically choked, wishing she could down the rest of the beer Jesse had taken from her.

"Yeah. I'm heading out on a red-eye tonight."

"How long are you going to be gone?"

"I don't know. No more than a day or two, I'm sure." He looked back to his friend. "Anyway, I was asking Kyle to keep an eye out for you." He gave an exaggerated wink. "You know, make sure no other guy makes a move on you."

Heidi took the beer from him and emptied it.

"What makes you think you can trust me with the job?" Kyle asked.

"I'm going to get more beer," Heidi said. "Anyone else want one?"

She knew it was a stupid question, but it allowed her to escape the two men who were bantering as if they hadn't a care in the world. As if she hadn't slept with both of them in a period of a little over seventy-two hours.

She sidled up to the bar, resting her elbow on the edge and rubbing her throbbing temple.

"What a tangled web we weave," Nina's voice sounded next to her.

She stared at her employer and friend. "What?" she croaked.

There was no possible way Nina could know. Was there? Heidi hadn't seen her since last night. And while there were security cameras on the front door of the store, and at each cashier's station, they normally weren't reviewed unless something had happened, so there was no reason to believe Kyle had been seen coming and going from BMC.

Her face felt hot. Even if he had been seen, there was no reason for anyone to assume that the two of them had slept together. Was there?

"How do you mean?" Heidi managed to ask.

"You didn't tell me you were catering this shindig. When you requested the day off, I thought you had course studies to catch up on."

It was all Heidi could do not to sag with relief.

"Excellent spread," Nina said. "You're really beginning to expand your menu."

"Mmm. I made a list of easier recipes that could be prepared in advance."

"Are you ready to take on wedding receptions yet?"

Heidi gaped at her friend. "Have you and Kevin finally set a date?"

Nina named a Saturday in August.

Heidi's mind filled with all the preparations that would have to be made. Menus drawn up, supplies ordered, temporary help hired…

She smiled. her relief at being given something to think about other than her heavy guilt was very welcome indeed.

"You thought I was talking about something else, didn't you?" Nina asked.

"I don't know what you mean," she lied.

"Don't give me that. Okay, Heidi, what else are you hiding from me?"

She flashed Nina a smile as she juggled three cups of beer. "I have no idea what you're talking about. See you later."

She walked away feeling tons better than she had moments ago.

And up to the task that lay ahead of her. Because if there was one thing she was determined to do, it was to reveal all to Jesse before he got on that plane tonight…

UNFORTUNATELY, the opportunity to talk to Jesse had never presented itself. Heidi had returned with the beer to find he'd finished his plate and had moved on to playing horseshoes with the guys. She knew better than to try to pull him away from group sports. So she'd hung back with the girls instead, waiting for an opening.

Only that opening had never come. When the time neared for his flight, he'd given her a kiss and said that Kyle was going to be driving him to the airport.

Heidi scrubbed at a pan that had been long past clean five minutes ago, every task seeming to take double the time as she wondered what the two friends discussed during the forty-five-minute drive to Detroit Metro Airport. Since Kyle had been tied up with Jesse, she hadn't had a chance to ask him what his plans were.

She plopped her hands into the water and stretched her tense neck. Damn it. She hated not having control over her life. What had ever inspired her to have a fling in the first place? She was more careful than that.

Perhaps *careful* wasn't the word she was looking for. Rather, she'd never been tempted to veer from her chosen path.

So why had she done so?

She rinsed the last of the pans and washed out the sink then stood at the counter staring out the back window into the dark yard. Fireflies pricked the darkness with brief flashes of yellow and somewhere a locust called out to its lover. A few days ago she would have gazed upon such a sight and imagined family barbecues much like the one she'd catered tonight…she and Jesse would have their own children, plus Jesse's large family, with perhaps her mother and sisters and their growing broods included.

Now…

Well, now a crack had appeared straight down the middle of that happy image, as if it were a pane of glass.

The telephone rang. She listlessly dried her hands on her short apron and reached for the receiver.

Her mother.

"Hi, mom."

"Hi yourself. How did everything go tonight?"

"Great. Everyone was happy."

"You don't sound happy."

"I'm just a little tired, I guess." She glanced at the clock to find it was near midnight. Which wasn't unusual for her mother. Alice called when the thought occurred to her, whether it was seven in the morning or as late as 1:00 a.m. "Is everything all right?" Heidi asked, just the same.

A heavy sigh then, "I'm having the opposite problem. I can't sleep."

"Try a mug of chamomile."

"In this heat?"

Heidi smiled, forgetting that her mother didn't like to turn on the rattling old air conditioner that blocked her bedroom window.

"Anyway, I was calling to see why you haven't come over here yet. If I didn't know better, I'd think you were avoiding me."

Story of her life. "No, no. Really. It's just that I've been so busy." She rubbed her forehead. "I'll try to get by tomorrow."

"How about now?"

"How about you tell me what's on your mind over the phone?"

"Nothing doing. This isn't the kind of news you share over the phone."

Heidi drew her brows together. News? Uh-oh. She didn't like the sound of this.

There was a soft knock on the front door. Now who in the hell could that be?

"What is it? Is Melody pregnant again? Oh, no, wait. Faith went and quit high school a year before graduation," she pondered aloud as she walked to the door.

"No, no, nothing like that," her mother said.

Heidi pushed the curtain on the door aside and nearly gasped.

Kyle.

"Um, Mom, I've got to go," she said, cringing when she realized she'd probably given something away. She could have just as easily said that she'd see her tomorrow. So she told her mother that and then hung up the phone, hoping against hope that Alice Joblowski wouldn't call back to see what was up.

Heidi pulled open the door and stood staring at an equally quiet and curious Kyle.

"I think we need to talk," he said.

Heidi pulled the door wider to let him in.

7

KYLE STUFFED his hands deep into his pockets and crossed the threshold into Heidi's summer rental house. The place smelled as though someone had been cooking, which, of course, she had.

"Did you get him to the airport all right?"

He nodded.

"And…"

He waited for her to finish. She didn't. Instead, she drew in a deep breath and untied her apron and turned toward the kitchen.

"Can I get you something? I have some fresh squeezed lemonade."

"Sounds good."

Kyle fought the desire to follow her. The last time they'd been alone in a kitchen together hadn't turned out well.

That wasn't entirely true. He supposed it depended on your definition of *well*. Because when all was said and done, and all the grueling little details pushed aside, Heidi had been the best sex he'd ever had.

He discovered he was staring into the bedroom. The bed was unmade and it was all too easy to remember the sight of her nude, lying against the white sheets.

Damn.

He ran his hand through his hair several times.

Heidi came out with two glasses of lemonade and a plate of cookies. He thought they might be left over from the barbecue earlier, but he didn't remember seeing either kind on the tables there.

She put his glass on the coffee table in front of the sofa along with the cookies, then sat down in a rocking chair off to the side. She looked tense and more than a little tired.

He sat down in the middle of the sofa, hating that the vantage point gave him a perfect view of the bedroom and an instant fantasy of taking her on that bed.

He cleared his throat. "Sorry to come over so late, but I figured since this was the only time we could be sure of where Jesse was, it might be a good time to discuss how you want to handle things."

Her eyebrows rose on her forehead.

He leaned his forearms against his knees and clasped his hands together. He noticed the way she watched the movement as if acutely aware of his every action.

He could relate. He was tuned in to everything she did. Earlier he'd watched her nicely shaped behind as she unwittingly wiggled it while retrieving utensils from under a table. And he'd barely been able to keep his gaze off the sway of her breasts as she stirred the potato salad.

"So you think this is my fault?" she asked.

"Pardon me?" He smiled at her, then stopped when he found she was serious. He looked at his hands. "No. I just thought that maybe you'd like to be the one to call the shots here, seeing you're probably the one with the most at risk."

She motioned for him to go on, but he was done.

He leaned back in the sofa and sipped the lemonade. "If you want me to talk to him, that's okay. I can own up to what happened."

"No, no. Please don't do that." Her face looked pinched and she sat back in her own chair, staring at the glass she held. "It sounds so sordid when you put it that way."

He nodded again.

She didn't say anything for long minutes, continuing to stare at her glass though she had yet to drink from it.

"Are you okay?" he asked.

"Hmm?" She looked at him and then shook her head. "I'm sorry. I seem to be doing that a lot today. Zoning out."

He'd noticed. Not that it had interfered with her duties as caterer. But he'd often caught her standing still, seeming lost in thought.

"This…I don't know. This just isn't something I do, you know?"

He gave a wry smile. "And you think I do?"

She considered him for a long moment. "I don't know you well enough to say one way or another. For all I know, you go around sleeping with all your friends' women."

He winced. "Ouch."

"Sorry." And she looked it. "I'm trying hard to make sense out of this and…"

He noticed the way her fingers tightened around her glass.

"And no matter how hard you try, it refuses to come together," he offered.

"Yes…"

Kyle fell silent for a few moments then quietly cleared his throat. "Have you considered that maybe there are some things that aren't meant to make sense? That they just…are?"

He felt her gaze on him but kept his focus on her hands.

"It happened. We can't change it." He glanced up at her now. "And I, for one, wouldn't change it. No matter what we're going through. No matter that my best friend is going to be hurt when he finds out. No matter the risk to myself and our friendship…"

"You wouldn't take it back?"

"You're forgetting that we *can't* take it back."

She put her glass down on the coffee table and gestured with her hands, her expression pensive. "I'm asking whether if you could, you wouldn't?"

He studied her for long, silent moments before answering. "No. I wouldn't."

He didn't ask her what she would do. He had the feeling she would change what had happened in an instant if she could. Turn the clock hands back to last night when they stood in the café's kitchen, and rather than kiss him, she would walk out the door.

How much easier things would be if they could do that.

How much duller.

Kyle had never thought himself an adventure junkie. Oh, some of his teenage behavior—and even college— might have been borderline rebellious, but he'd never done anything of this nature before.

"Bros before hos." That was the motto between him and his friends, meaning friendship before women always. And one canon you never violated was dating a friend's old flame…much less a current one.

He rubbed his face, the scratching of his palms against his stubble reminding him of the late hour.

He rose from the sofa. "I'd better get going."

Heidi made no effort to stop him. At least no outward effort. But the softness of her eyes and the disappointment that bracketed her mouth told him much more than probably even she would like to betray.

Kyle forced himself to walk to the door.

"About that party…"

She blinked as if not getting what he'd said.

"The birthday party for Jesse. I was thinking this might be a good time to iron out the rest of the details, while he's away. Divide up the chores…"

"Oh." Heidi held open the door. "Yes. It probably would." She caught her bottom lip between her straight white teeth and sighed. "I can probably get Jesse's sisters to help. They love doing this kind of thing."

Kyle nodded. "Good idea."

It struck him as odd that he hadn't thought of that before.

Why hadn't he gone to Jesse's three older sisters before approaching Heidi? He knew them well enough. And as Heidi suggested, they enjoyed arranging events like this. The Gilbred sisters were famous for their parties.

Instead he'd gone to Heidi.

"Well then…goodnight."

It was his turn to blink his mind back on track. "Oh. Right."

He gazed down at her one last time. Was it him, or had her pupils just expanded, large dark pools in her light brown eyes? He noticed his own heightened awareness of her, from the subtle scent of her skin, to the soft whoosh of her breathing...

If she were anyone else, he would have kissed her. More than that, he would have backed her toward the couch until she fell across it, and he would have followed, never breaking the contact of their mouths. He would have cupped her breast through the soft cotton of her shirt and wedged his knee between her jeans-clad thighs. He would have kissed her for hours, leaving them both breathless and panting with need.

But she wasn't anyone else. She was Heidi Joblowski. She was Jesse's girl.

Kyle cleared his throat and walked through the door, listening as it closed quietly behind him.

THE MAGIC HOUR. Heidi remembered reading somewhere that that's what photographers called the few hours before dusk, when the sun washed everything in a warm, golden, almost surreal light. Especially the summer sun, which had transformed the sky into a Monet painting come to life.

The light somehow managed to make even the shabby, one-story two-bedroom house on the outskirts of Fantasy look better. Quaint, even. Which was definitely not the way she'd have described the place growing up. The words others used to describe her and her family were more along the lines of *white trash, deadbeats, welfare children.*

She took in the peeling paint that was more gray than white, the overgrown, patchy grass, the drooping, unkempt morning glories on one side of the bowed, wooden stairs. She knew exactly where the wood would groan when she stepped on it, how the old aluminum screen door would clap shut when she went inside. She would recognize the musty smell of the interior of the old house, which probably wouldn't pass a health inspection should the city be interested in looking at it.

She'd spent most of her life trying to forget that this was where she was from. To forget the names she and her mother and sisters were called.

But as soon as she got close to achieving her objective, she would visit again and be sucked back in time. Which didn't happen all that often. She and her mother were pretty good at keeping up their relationship via the telephone and monthly dinners out and the occasional movie, meeting at the theater so Heidi could pretend not to notice the old rusty Cadillac her mother drove.

Readjusting her hold on the bag of leftovers from the barbecue last night, she climbed the steps, almost immediately hearing her mother's voice from inside.

"Heidi!" she called. "Come in, come in." She held the door open and Heidi ducked under her arm to enter. "My, my. Aren't you a sight for sore eyes? You're looking good, girl. But of course, you would. You inherited your mama's good genes, after all."

Heidi suppressed an eye roll, having heard the same greeting nearly every time she saw her mother. And Alice always expected for her to react as though it was the first time.

"I brought some food over. Some of it needs to be refrigerated." She led the way into the kitchen and put the bag on the old yellow Formica table, which was surrounded by three mismatched chairs and a baby's high chair that had long since lost its tray and been pulled up to the table.

The only saving grace was that the place was clean. Her mother was steadfast about that. "I might not have much, but I take care of what I have" was one of her favorite sayings as she scrubbed the kitchen floor or hand-washed the faded front-window curtains.

Her mother leaned against the kitchen counter and crossed her arms over her tank top and jeans shorts, watching Heidi as she took the things out of the bag and opened the refrigerator door.

"Are the Sampsons moving?" Heidi asked, having seen a for sale sign in front of the house across the street.

Alice sighed. "Yeah. Got a second mortgage from one of those disreputable companies that turned around and jacked up the interest on them. They can't afford the payments no more, what with that boy of theirs having gotten into that accident and all."

Heidi opened the top of an almost-empty milk carton, sniffed it and then tossed it into the garbage can nearby. "What accident?"

"Didn't I tell you? They let him buy one of those dirt bikes a few months back when spring sprung—"

"How old is he now?" The last time Heidi remembered seeing him, he couldn't have been more than seven.

"Fifteen. Anyway, like the fools most fifteen-year-old boys are, he was out riding that death trap around the neighborhood, didn't stop at the sign a block up, and was knocked thirty feet into the air. Lost his right foot."

Heidi stared at her mother from over the refrigerator door.

"God's honest truth. As soon as he heals well enough they're going to fit him with one of those bionic things…"

Heidi rolled her eyes behind the safety of the door as she finished tossing out the rotting or rotten food and replacing it with what she'd brought. If she were to come back next week, she'd probably have to toss that food, as well. Alice Joblowski had always said that eating fast food was cheaper than making her own.

The unfortunate part was that she was probably right.

Heidi took out two sodas and closed the door, holding out a can for her mother. She hadn't caught the last two minutes of Alice's monologue but gathered that the kid had found a way to get ahold of some drugs and his mother was worried he might kill himself and maybe this move might be good for him, get him away from his old life so they could start a new one because nothing was going to be the same for him again anyway.

As Heidi sipped her cola and stared at her mother, she wondered why she hadn't inherited Alice's gift for gab as well as her supposedly "attractive" genes. Then again, she didn't remember many opportunities for conversation. If her mother wasn't talking a mile a minute, she had her nose buried in one of her library books. Heidi looked around and, sure enough, found the latest bestseller, with a ruler stuck in it as a bookmark, on the counter next to her mother. She'd probably been reading it when Heidi came up the front walk.

"What I want to know," her mother said, crossing her arms under her breasts again, "is how you lost *your* foot?"

8

AN HOUR later, Heidi was still asking herself how her mother managed to do that. One minute she was going on and on about a neighbor boy whom Heidi hadn't seen in ages, the next she was using his experience as a measuring stick against her daughter's life.

How'd she lose her own foot? indeed.

Of course, her mother had been speaking metaphorically. She guessed—rightly so—that Heidi had indulged in dangerous behavior and the consequence was not the loss of a body part, but something equally important: her own respect.

She didn't dare tell Alice what was going on. She was half afraid she'd tell her to bring Kyle around for dinner.

Okay, so her mother and Jesse didn't get along. Or, rather, her mother didn't like Jesse and he...well, it wasn't that he didn't like her mother. It was more that he hadn't taken the time to get to know her, mostly because Heidi made sure their paths didn't often cross.

Why was that?

It might have something to do with her own reluctance to be reminded of her past.

Might? That was the entire reason her mother and

Jesse didn't see each other much. Because Heidi didn't see her own mother, even though they only lived a few miles from each other.

But she was getting way off topic. Mentally babbling the same way that her mother was literally babbling.

"Your sister Melody has moved in again."

Heidi looked at the high chair next to her. "I guessed."

Alice sighed. "Yeah, she and Johnny are having a hard time of it. Little Tyler is not even three yet and he's known more homes than a full-grown adult."

Heidi lifted her face so that the rattling old fan on the counter could hit her hot skin with air. She supposed she could be thankful that she'd at least lived in the same house her entire life. But that was only because her mother had gotten the house in the divorce settlement from Heidi's father and had been damn lucky she hadn't lost it like the Sampsons were losing theirs.

"Where is she?" Heidi asked.

"Down at the welfare office straightening out a few things."

Where else would her sister be? Certainly not looking for work. Melody was known for finding jobs quickly, and losing them just as quickly for reasons that were never her fault. Her car had broken down, or her ride couldn't bring her in, or the water bill was due, or she had to take the baby in for a checkup. There was always some reason why Mel was late or absent, putting her employers in a bind and then herself when she ultimately lost the jobs.

"Is that why you called me to come over?" Heidi asked. "Does the news have something to do with Melody?"

Her mother craned her head, watching through the

window as a car pulled into the neighbor's driveway. It sounded as if it was steering itself directly into her own kitchen.

"Oh, my God," Heidi said, measuring her mother's reluctance. "Don't tell me. Melody's pregnant again."

She groaned, feeling as if the air had been sucked from the room.

"Don't be silly. Melody's not pregnant." Her mother rolled her eyes. "What would make you think that?"

Heidi released a long sigh of relief.

"She's not pregnant. I am…"

A RERUN of Conan O'Brien played in the living room as Heidi sat in her own kitchen, her feet propped up on an opposite chair, staring at the doodles she'd made on the pad in front of her. They outnumbered the party details she'd planned to make two to one.

Her mother was pregnant. Her forty-two-year-old, unmarried, unemployed mother was pregnant with her sixth child. A child that would be Heidi's younger brother or sister. A child that would be uncle to Melody's son, even though Tyler would be older than him.

She plopped her elbow on the table and rested her forehead in her hand, groaning loudly.

"Of course I won't give it up!" her mother had nearly shouted at Heidi's suggestion. "My being pregnant means I was meant to have another kid."

"No, Mom, it means that you, more than anyone, should have been using contraception. My God, do you know how many STDs you can catch? Not to mention that HIV/AIDS hasn't exactly been cured yet."

"Heidi, I'm pregnant. Not dying."

No, her mother wasn't dying. But she was doing her damnedest to chase Heidi to an early grave.

Her…mother…was…pregnant.

She listlessly picked up her cell phone from the table to make sure she had the ringer on. It was on. Just as it had been the last three times she'd checked.

She sighed and put it back down. She'd left three messages for Jesse and he had yet to call back. She needed to confide in somebody about this whole fiasco. Someone who would reassure her that she wasn't cold to think that her mother shouldn't be bringing another child into this world.

"Do you even know who the father is?"

Her mother had looked affronted. "Of course I do. I know the fathers of all my children."

No, she'd known the sperm donors, not fathers. Because one actually had to have performed the job of "fathering" to qualify for the title. And aside from the odd Christmas card and birthday gift, and her mother's monthly child support checks, neither she nor her sisters had really had a true father figure.

It broke her heart to think that the same fate awaited her mother's sixth child.

She groaned again and laid her forehead on the table. She would have felt less upset if it had been her sister who was pregnant, not their mother.

The cell chirped. She scrambled to pick up, nearly dropping it before finally answering.

"Hey, babe. You rang?"

She instantly relaxed. Jesse. "Yes. Three times."

"Sorry. They took me out to dinner and you know

how these things can get." She heard noise in the background that sounded like a bar.

"That's all right. I just needed to hear your voice, that's all."

This was the point where Jesse would usually say something along the lines of, "Is everything all right?" Or perhaps she was projecting her needs onto him.

What she got instead was, "The guys are calling me back. I've got to go. Call you tomorrow?"

For a moment Heidi was at a loss for words, then she said, "Sure, sure. Of course. I didn't mean to interrupt."

He blew her air kisses and then hung up.

Heidi stared at the cell phone screen for long moments then pressed the disconnect button on her end.

She hadn't meant to interrupt? Had she really just said that? Of course she'd meant to interrupt.

Then she remembered Kyle and groaned all over again.

God, she'd completely forgotten about that.

Hadn't she?

Yes, she realized. She had. In light of her mother's news, she'd completely overlooked her own sexual activities over the past couple of days.

She could only thank God that she and Kyle had used protection. Because if she truly was her mother's daughter, she would have ended up pregnant with Kyle's baby while engaged to Jesse.

Now that was a thought worth keeping up front and prominent in her mind.

The cell chirped again. Jesse.

She quickly answered, thankful that he must have heard the distress in her voice and was calling back from a more private location.

"Hey," another male voice said instead.

Kyle.

"Hey, yourself," Heidi said. She glanced around the kitchen, waiting for him to say something. Anything that would make the ache in the pit of her stomach go away.

She squinted. "Look, Kyle, I have a lot to do. Is there something that you wanted?"

She snapped her mouth tightly shut so she wouldn't give in to the desire building within her to invite him over, to transfer the heavy burden from her shoulders onto his.

"From what I can see, you're not doing anything."

Heidi's head shot up and she automatically reached to pull down the hem of the short nightie she had on, taking her feet off the other chair. "Where are you?"

She saw movement outside the door leading to the backyard and slapped a hand to her chest.

"Jesus, you scared the hell out of me."

"I told you I could see you."

"I know, but…"

"May I come in?"

"Are you stalking me?"

"I'm not stalking you." He held up something in the window. "Jesse's sisters made up this book of possible menus, decorating schemes, music possibilities and, well, I was hoping you might go through them with me."

Heidi moved to stand on the other side of the door, the phone cupped to her ear as she stared at both her own reflection in the glass and Kyle on the other side of it.

He looked good. Too good.

And she was feeling unnaturally weak.

Not that weakness had led to her having sex with him. But now that she had been intimate with him, she was terrified that if she opened the door, the temptation to melt into his arms and let him carry her off to the bedroom would be too great for her to resist.

"You look good," Kyle said quietly.

She smiled and looked down. "So do you."

"So open the door so I can see you better."

Heidi stood for long moments, feeling the cold of the air conditioning inside even as she imagined the thick, wet heat outside. If she opened the door she'd be letting the heat in, both figuratively and literally. A type of heat that couldn't be taken care of with the simple press of a button. She'd be allowing it to swirl around her, to slip inside her, to consume her inside and out.

She tightly closed her eyes. The image of her mother smiling warmly and caressing her still-flat stomach gave her strength. "No. In the annals of bad ideas, opening this door would rank right at the top."

Her palm felt damp against the cell as she lifted her gaze to his.

"I was afraid you'd say that."

"Well, what did you expect me to do? Welcome you in with open legs?"

His grin was unmistakable. "No. But I was hoping open arms might not be outside the realm of possibility."

She laughed quietly and leaned her shoulder against the door frame, her nose mere inches from the glass. "You're incorrigible, has anyone ever told you that?"

"Yes. You. Just now."

He'd moved closer to the door, and despite the glass separating them, they were close enough to kiss. Which made Heidi doubly glad that the barrier was there.

Kyle leaned in and huffed a breath against his side of the pane. Heidi watched, fascinated. He lifted a finger and wrote something there that she couldn't make out because the words were backward, meant to be read on his side.

"So," he said, stepping back. "I guess I should be going then."

"Yes," Heidi forced herself to say.

"Okay." He started down the stairs to the walk that led around to the driveway. "How about I stop by the café tomorrow for lunch?"

"No!" She sighed at her overreaction. "Just leave the book on the steps. I'll, um, call you with my thoughts."

"And then you'll leave it on the steps of my place?"

Sounded like a good plan to her. She nodded.

"Fine," he said, and bent over to put the book down.

"Thanks."

"Don't mention it."

He stood for a long moment, staring at her through the darkness. Then he slowly removed the cell from his ear, the keyboard momentarily illuminating his profile in neon blue. He closed the phone and turned and disappeared down the walk.

Heidi stood silently, closing her own phone. Headlights reflected off the one-car garage to her right and then receded as Kyle backed out of the driveway. She leaned her head against the cool glass. What was he doing? Did he know that her nerves were already stretched beyond breaking? That every time she saw him, it was that much more difficult to keep herself from touching him? And now with Jesse gone…

She pressed her fingertips against her closed eyelids until she saw stars. What was she talking about? If she loved Jesse, she wouldn't have to worry about the temptation of touching anyone else, let alone his best friend.

She checked to make sure no headlights still shone in the drive, then she unlocked the back door and stepped outside. She opened her mouth to huff against the glass where he'd written something, then cursed herself, paced a few steps away, and then came back again.

Oh, screw it.

She breathed against the glass once more, revealing the words Good Night.

She smiled, looking in the direction he'd gone. He'd known she wasn't going to let him in. But he'd tried anyway.

"Good night," she whispered into the dark, thick summer air.

9

"HEIDI! How great to see you. Come in, come in." Jesse's sister Annie opened the door of her McMansion, located in the latest housing development, and motioned for Heidi to enter. She had eight-month-old Mason on her hip while two-and-a-half-year-old Jasmine stood behind her, her hand fisted in the back of Annie's capris.

Heidi cooed at Mason and asked Jaz how she was doing, coaxing a giggle out of her before Annie led the way back to the kitchen.

"Both Liz and I thought it was a great idea, you know, throwing a birthday party for Jesse, when Kyle brought it up. I don't know why we hadn't thought about it. I mean, it is the big twenty-five and all."

Heidi hoisted Jaz up and stared into her big, blue eyes. "I think these two are reason enough to forget what color the sky is."

Annie laughed. "You can say that again." She put Mason in his high chair and then leaned closer. "It's not common knowledge yet, so it's not for general consumption, but I'm three months along on our next."

Heidi raised her brows. "I thought you wanted to stop at two."

"I did, too." Annie rubbed her stomach. "But seems

this one in here had other ideas. Iced tea okay?" Heidi said it was. "We Gilbreds are a fertile bunch."

They weren't the only ones. Her own family appeared not to know how to turn sperm away, either.

The thought caught her unawares. Especially considering that her feelings toward Annie's reproductive habits and her own mother's couldn't have been more different.

That was odd. Wasn't it?

Annie peeked around the refrigerator door. "I think it's important you know that, what with you and Jesse about to tie the knot and all."

"Know what?"

Annie raised her brows. "How fertile the Gilbreds are—men *and* women." She laughed. "Although when it comes to Jesse the correct term would be *virile*."

Heidi was glad Annie had busied herself adding ice to two glasses and then filling them with tea from a pitcher, because she wasn't sure what her expression might have revealed.

How strange everything seemed suddenly. It wasn't long ago that a visit like this would have been comfortable and comforting. For what seemed like forever she'd used Annie's life as a blueprint for the one she wanted. Marriage. Kids. And while Annie had taken a break from her career as an attorney, she'd been, and no doubt would be again, very successful. She and her husband, Roger, had a beautiful new house, and all seemed to be coming up roses for the couple and their young family.

The telephone rang and Annie picked it up. The loud sound must have startled little Mason and he began crying, while Jaz had taken to tugging on her mother's pants in need of something Heidi couldn't make out over Mason's wails.

Just last month during a Saturday family barbecue, Heidi had sat back with an impossible smile pasted on her face as she watched Annie and her family, imagining her and Jesse making a similar picture three or four years down the road.

Now…

She squinted at Annie. Was it her imagination, or did her future sister-in-law look as though she needed sleep? Was her smile a little tight? Did she know that there was a cracker lying in the corner of the floor or that the fern over the kitchen sink needed to be watered?

"I can't deal with this right now, Roger. Why do you always do this to me? I'm not raising my voice, you are. Fine. We'll talk later."

Pretending she couldn't hear Annie's side of the conversation with her husband, Heidi picked Mason up and bounced him, wiping the wetness from his cheeks. He stopped crying, and she turned to see what she could do about Jaz, only to find that Annie had hung up the phone and was standing clutching the counter as she stared out the back window, her knuckles white. The two-year-old continued tugging on her capris but Annie appeared not to notice.

"Annie?" Heidi said quietly, putting Mason back in his chair and handing him his teething ring.

The blonde made a sound as if surprised to find she wasn't alone and quickly wiped her cheeks.

"Men," Annie said with forced cheerfulness as she turned back toward Heidi. Jaz followed and Heidi swooped her up and took a seat at the counter, setting the little girl on her lap. "I swear, if they're not complaining about getting enough sex, they're making some other impossible request."

Heidi's brows shot up on her forehead.

Annie tried to laugh it off. "Never mind me. I'm a train wreck of runaway hormones right now." She put a glass of iced tea in front of Heidi and then took a sip of her own. "I haven't even told Roger yet."

"Told him what? About the baby?"

Annie tipped her head. "Yeah. I've known for three days. I keep waiting for the perfect time to tell him and, well…as you could hear from the phone call, those particular times seem to be few and far between lately." She absently scratched at a spot on the counter. "Maybe tonight."

Heidi looked at the little girl in her lap. She was staring at her mother with the same wide-eyed expression that Heidi suspected she herself wore.

She began to suggest that perhaps she should babysit that night before her class, take the kids to her place or out to the park for a little while to give Annie a breather, when the front doorbell rang.

"Oh! I almost forgot."

Annie edged around the island.

"Lizzie couldn't make it because she's working, but I invited Kyle to go over the final details with us." She gave Heidi a dramatic wink. "We can give Liz all the drudge work."

Heidi must have squeezed Jaz a little too hard because the girl gave a squeak and demanded to be let down.

KYLE HADN'T SMOKED in over five years, but as he watched Heidi back out of Annie's driveway as if the very devil were nipping at her heels, he craved a cigarette in the worst way.

"She seemed distracted," Annie said from beside him.

He grimaced. "Yeah, she did, didn't she?"

"It's probably because Jesse's away on that business trip. I'm always a mess when Roger travels."

Kyle looked at Jesse's sister. "Yeah, that's probably it."

But he knew it wasn't. Things had evolved to become more than friendly between him and Heidi. And neither of them had a clue what to do about it.

OKAY, that definitely hadn't gone as planned.

After the meeting at Annie's, Heidi felt as if she existed in some sort of alternative reality. She recognized the landmarks, yet somehow nothing looked the way it ought to look.

Kyle…

Merely thinking his name made her feel warm all over—the type of heat that didn't have anything to do with the day's high temperatures, but rather her own internal thermometer, which recently seemed to nudge up whenever she was within touching distance of him.

As she walked from her night class to the student parking lot, she groaned loudly.

She was thankful that Annie seemed to be distracted by the state of her own life and hadn't noticed the glances Heidi and Kyle shared. At one point, however, little Jasmine had tuned in with the laser-like precision that only children possessed and had tugged on Kyle's arm, telling him, "Stop looking at Aunt Heidi and play with me."

Heidi had nearly choked with embarrassment.

In her purse, she felt the vibration of her cell phone. She fished it out, not recognizing the number.

"Hello?"

"Heidi? Thank God you picked up."

Jesse.

Her throat threatened to close.

"Look, I lost my cell phone so I'm calling you on the air phone—"

"Air phone?"

"Yeah, you know, those twenty-dollar-a-minute things on the plane? Anyway, I need you to pick me up. The plane will be landing in Detroit in an hour. Can you do it?"

"Sure."

"Good. See you then. Thanks, babe."

He hung up.

Heidi slowly closed her phone. It took three tries before she blindly stuffed it back into her purse, where she wished she had left it. Even then, she had to check to make sure she hadn't dropped it on the ground.

Crap.

She should have asked why Kyle wasn't picking him up. Should have told him she had a class. Then again, he knew her schedule, or should, so that excuse might have backfired on her.

She discovered she was dragging her feet and forced herself to quicken her steps. She'd have to hurry if she was going to get to the airport in time to meet Jesse's flight.

She wondered if it weren't too late to call Kyle and

ask him to do it. But the thought of talking to him so soon after seeing him at Annie's might be the end of her.

Besides, for all she knew, Jesse had called Kyle and he hadn't been able to make the drive for whatever reason.

And then there was the whole excuse angle again.

I got a flat tire…

My mother needed to see me…

I'm a veritable basket case because I've slept with your best friend once and oh, but oh, would I love to do it again…

What a mess.

"I want to kiss you."

Kyle's softly spoken words in Annie's pantry a few hours earlier made her shiver all over again.

"Damn my soul to hell, Heidi, but it's all I can think about. Kissing you again."

She'd gone in to get a can of SpaghettiOs for Jaz's lunch while Annie took Mason up for his nap, and Kyle had followed without her knowing. Until she felt his warm breath on the back of her neck.

"No, don't," he said, his body making contact with hers. "If you turn around, I'll kiss you."

Heidi had caught her breath and closed her eyes, wanting the very same thing.

And she still did.

What was she going to do? Was it possible to want two men at the same time? And even if it was, there was nowhere for her to go with this. She'd come too far with Jesse to think about turning back now. Soon they would be engaged, married, and living a life like his sister Annie and Roger's.

That caught her up short in light of her discovery today that Camelot had its own unique land mines.

She shook her head. It didn't matter. She wanted this. Had grown up wanting this. And she was so close to having it she could taste it.

And what about Kyle?

What about Kyle, indeed.

Should he stay in the picture, it would mean crossing paths with him often. From softball games, to fall touch football games, NFL Sundays and hockey Saturdays, and basketball every days…her heartbeat quickened at the idea that she'd be seeing the sexy architect almost as much as she'd see Jesse.

How would Kyle feel about that? If she finally drew the line and insisted he stop coming on to her, would he respect her wishes? Or would he see through the crack in her armor and accept it as a challenge to see how far he had to go to strip her of it completely?

"It'll pass," she whispered to herself as she reached the student parking lot and pressed the remote to unlock her door.

What was she talking about? She wasn't suffering from some sort of nymphomaniacal flu that could be taken care of with a bit of chicken soup, bed rest and time.

Then again, time might just be the ticket in this situation. Just as time healed all wounds, so did it cool burning embers. The fire that had flamed up between them could be banked and put out altogether.

Of course, she was forgetting one little detail. The fact that Jesse might not forgive either one of them for their betrayal.

She sat in the car tightly gripping the steering wheel, her mind a complete blank.

And for the first time she considered never telling Jesse.

10

OKAY, so maybe the idea not to tell Jesse anything wasn't a good one. Truth was, she'd never been very adept at lying. And she didn't want to start now. If she and Jesse were going to have a future together, they needed to do it with a clean slate.

So then why was she wasting time in the kitchen cooking a complicated meal that could have been kept simple?

Heidi didn't want to examine that question too closely for fear of what she'd come away with. So she was scared. She should be. She'd put so much on the line with that one night of passion. And now it was time to pay the piper.

She transferred the freshly cooked pasta into the truffle sauce and then turned down the fire under the pan, flipping it to mix the ingredients. She was too pre-occupied to enjoy the smell.

"Hey, babe. Glad you could make it."

Those were Jesse's words when he'd climbed into her car after stowing his suitcase in the trunk. He'd given her a brief, perfunctory kiss and then gestured which direction was the best to take from the airport.

The forty-five-minute drive home had been filled

with conversation about his travel tribulations and hotel problems and the like.

"I tried calling you at the hotel. They told me you never checked in."

Jesse had blinked at her as if he didn't know what she meant, and then he'd snapped his fingers. "Of course. I changed reservations to a hotel where some of the other guys were staying. Sorry if I worried you."

"I *was* worried," she told him. But she had been curious, too.

Heidi switched off the heat and quickly transferred the pasta to two large bowls. She wiped her hands on her apron and took in the results of the past hour. Fresh garlic breadsticks, a large salad and pasta along with a nice chianti and two wineglasses on the kitchen table. She'd also placed two candles there, but now she blew them out and put the candles on the counter.

She had to tell Jesse the truth.

Speaking of Jesse, where was he?

She took off her apron and hung it on the doorknob as she left the kitchen. He'd gone to take a shower when they'd returned and she hadn't seen him since.

She walked to the bedroom, stopping in the doorway. There in front of her was Jesse, lying diagonally across the bed, dead to the world.

Hmmph.

And to think her greatest fear was that he would want sex, seeing as they'd been apart for three days.

She crossed the room and sat on the side of the mattress, taking in his fine form against her white duvet. He wore nothing but a pair of boxers, his hair still wet from the shower. He looked so boyish when he slept.

As if he hadn't a care in the world. Then again, that's the way he always looked. Rarely was the time when you'd catch Jesse with his brow creased, or a frown weighing down his well-defined mouth. He was always smiling and ready for fun.

Heidi fingered the curls at his nape, her heart hurting at the thought that her actions might change that.

She leaned in. "Jesse?"

He barely budged. "Hmm?"

"Dinner's ready."

"Mmm."

He turned his head away from her and settled more fully into the bedding.

She smiled. "That's all right. You just go ahead and sleep."

She took a chenille throw from the corner chair and draped it over him, then looked at her watch. Just after eleven.

Now what the hell was she going to do?

She headed to the kitchen and picked a couple of truffles from the sauce she'd made, then sat at the table alone, chewing on a breadstick. She could always put dinner away and join Jesse in bed. He was so deeply asleep that she doubted she'd waken him.

Problem was, she wasn't tired.

She cleared the table and stood staring at the flan she'd made. Without caramelizing the top, she carried the dessert into the living room. She closed the bedroom door so she wouldn't disturb Jesse and then curled up on the couch and flicked on the television with the remote. She must have left it on a cable channel and a particularly erotic image from the movie *Unfaithful* took her breath away. These things never ended well. Didn't Richard Gere kill the yummy Olivier Martinez at the end of that movie? She quickly changed the channel, not needing any more fuel to add to her own personal fire.

She settled on the news, which would be followed by Letterman, and absently ate her flan. It felt as if some sort of clock was ticking. Loudly. And the longer she put off telling Jesse, the louder that clock got.

She looked at her watch again and put the flan down, the creamy concoction tasting like grit against her guilty tongue.

She sighed deeply and picked up the novel she was reading, but after she'd read the same paragraph four times without comprehending the content, she gave up on that, too, and cuddled down into the sofa cushions.

Oh, screw it.

She switched the channel back to the movie…and fell asleep somewhere near the end, causing her to have all sorts of strange and frightening nightmares.

SHE AWAKENED the following morning to find Jesse already gone, a Post-it note on her bedroom mirror—Gotta run, babe. See you at the game? It had been signed simply, J.

Heidi crumpled the note with one hand and tossed it into the garbage. With her other hand she tried to work the kinks out of her neck caused by sleeping in an awkward position on the couch.

She took a quick shower to get ready for class and was just drying off when her cell phone rang in the other room. She rushed to get it, thinking it might be Jesse.

"Heidi?"

Not Jesse.

She swallowed hard. "Kyle."

"Did you pick up Jesse last night?"

"Of course I picked up Jesse. The question is why you didn't."

Silence. She realized she was still wet and awkwardly continued drying herself off while juggling the cell.

"Did you tell him?"

Heidi nearly dropped the phone.

There was silence for a moment, then she finally said, "Can you hold a minute?"

He indicated that he would and she tossed the phone to the middle of her bed and returned to the bathroom to finish drying off. She stood in front of the mirror and stared at her nude reflection, wondering just who the person staring back at her was. Her hair was still wet and she'd combed it back. The style brought her angular features into relief, made her look edgy rather than sweet. She worked gel into it, then quickly dressed and picked up the phone on her way to the kitchen, where she'd put on coffee to brew.

"I take it that means no," Kyle said when she thanked him for holding.

"You take it right."

He was quiet as she poured her coffee, forgoing her usual cream and sugar and trying it black. She liked it. She opened the back door and sat on the step, the summer air warm against her skin.

"I'm going to see him this morning for a meeting," Kyle said.

"You plan on making the announcement a bullet on your agenda?"

"I'm not planning anything. But at this point, I think we both have to accept that it's going to come out sooner or later. One of us will let something slip."

"I agree."

"So do you have any suggestions?"

Heidi took a long sip of coffee and leaned back on her hand. "Beyond making an appointment with Jesse and telling him straight out…no."

"That's an option, you know."

Oh, she knew. And as things were going, it might just be what they needed to do.

"He stayed at your place last night?"

Kyle's question appeared casual enough. But considering their conversation, Heidi knew it wasn't.

"Yes," she said quietly.

She should have left it there. Let Kyle think that she and Jesse had slept together. After all, they had. At least under the same roof, if not in the same bed. And not in the biblical sense.

"He conked out in the bedroom while I was making dinner. I fell asleep on the couch. When I woke up this morning, he was gone."

She heard his sound of relief and tucked her chin into her chest, finding it impossible not to smile.

"Have lunch with me today."

Heidi's smile faded. "What?"

"You heard me. Meet me somewhere. I don't care. We can drive down to Toledo if you'd like, someplace where we won't run into anybody if that's what you want."

The suggestion was so outrageous to Heidi that she couldn't respond.

"I need to see you."

"Kyle…"

"I know. It's crazy, isn't it?"

She worried her bottom lip. "What if I hadn't told you that Jesse and I didn't sleep together last night?"

"I don't know."

That was honest enough, she supposed.

She took a deep breath and pressed the heel of her hand against her brow. "I don't think either of us should even think about doing anything together until we tell Jesse the truth."

"And where are we with that truth now?"

"What do you mean where are we? The truth isn't something that evolves or changes. It just is."

"Are you sure?"

"Look, Kyle, you're not making much sense, so I'm going to hang up now. Oh, and no to lunch. Go ask someone who's free."

KYLE SLOWLY hung up his office phone and sat back, his chair springs giving a soft creak. Damn it. This thing had gone much farther than he'd intended. He shouldn't have called Heidi. Shouldn't have asked her whether Jesse had stayed the night at her place. He knew he had because he'd gone by the place Jesse shared with two other guys and they said he hadn't come home from Boston yet.

Which meant he had to be at Heidi's.

The thought had driven him to distraction all night. He'd gone for a run at midnight, hoping to exorcise his demons through physical activity, but it hadn't worked. So instead he'd gone into his study and focused on his latest project, a building in Sylvania that would house a medical group. Forty offices with waiting areas, an employee track and gym on the second floor. Thankfully he was able to throw himself into the project and had exhausted himself by four o'clock.

But while he'd managed to calm his conscious mind, his unconscious took over.

Damn it, but he wanted Heidi—in every way it was possible to want a woman.

And she refused even to consider the possibility.

There had been few times in his life when his choices had been laid out clearly for him. He'd known he wanted to be an architect when his interest in building his savings had turned into an interest in building things that lasted. He'd known he and Jesse would be lifelong friends from the first moment they met.

And he knew he wanted Heidi.

He didn't appreciate the irony that when the truth came out he'd lose one or the other. Or quite possibly both.

He rubbed his closed eyelids with his thumbs. Whatever was going to happen had to happen now. He couldn't go one more night the way things were.

11

HEIDI JUGGLED a tray of hors d'oeuvres with a bag of rolls and used her elbow to hold open the door to the nursing home. She'd taken on the catering job to celebrate the one-hundredth birthday of one of the residents some months ago, and she'd planned the menu accordingly. Which meant fixing new foods she wasn't accustomed to fixing. But that went with the territory, didn't it? There were going to be requests made that wouldn't always be her specialty and she would have to adapt.

Only she hadn't anticipated having to work oatmeal and bran into so many of today's lunch offerings.

Someone caught the door and she nearly fell inside.

"May I be of help, miss?" asked an elderly gentleman wearing a blue-and-white checked shirt under a green sweater vest. He was holding his walker to one side as he propped the door open for her.

"Thanks. That should do it."

"You'd be surprised what I can balance on this thing," he said with a wink, gesturing toward his walker.

Heidi laughed. "I'm sure I would, but if I let go of one thing I'll lose the whole load."

Story of her life as of late, wasn't it?

"Where's the day room?" she asked.

"Down the hall and to your right. Why don't I lead the way?"

Heidi opened her mouth to tell him that she could handle it, but he whipped ahead of her before she could get out the first word.

Fine. They'd walk to the room at a snail's pace and she'd probably spill the contents of her tray anyway.

"Actually, I think I will take you up on your offer to show me just how well you can balance things on your walker," she said, adjusting her game plan.

The man looked around. "We'd have to go into one of the rooms with a door that closes."

Heidi gaped at him.

He chuckled good-naturedly. "Just kidding. Kids these days. Sexism and inappropriate behavior and all that. You would think that after the sixties, nothing would be off limits. You guys just don't know how to have a good time anymore."

He helped her put her tray on top of the walker and didn't complain when she kept her hand on it so it wouldn't fall as they wheeled their way down the long corridor.

"Now in my day, we knew how to have fun."

"Oh?" When Heidi saw that he had the tray positioned securely she moved her hard away.

"Post World War Two we knew what it was like to live in a world that could end at any moment. But you…you kids seem to forget that—bam!—it could all be over in the blink of an eye."

"Basile! Are you pestering the visitors again?" a handsome woman in a nurse's uniform asked as she came out of one of the offices.

"I'm helping the young lady," Basile insisted.

"I bet you are." The nurse leaned closer to Heidi. "If you feel any phantom pinches, he's the first one to look to."

Heidi raised her brows.

"Hi, I'm Mrs. Williams," the nurse said. "I'm the one who arranged the party for Mr. Savalas."

"Heidi Joblowski," she said.

"Joblowski?" Basile asked. "I served with a Joblowski. What's your grandfather's name?"

"I couldn't say."

Mrs. Williams gave Basile a stern look. "Heidi, I'd like you to meet one of our more active tenants, Basile—"

"We've met," he said. "Come on, Heidi. We have a date with the day room."

Heidi laughed and shared a look of commiseration with the nurse before following him into the day room. Despite the walker, Basile didn't look a day older than eighty. He was a couple of inches taller than she was and stocky, his white hair full and longish, further emphasizing his tanned face and flirty grin.

She saw that the serving tables had already been set up, which was a relief. Some clients seemed to think that if they weren't sure how you wanted things, it was best just to let you do it yourself. The tables even had linens on them, so she wouldn't have to use her own. She could just decorate them with some ivy and flowers.

"Where do you want this?"

Heidi accepted the tray from Basile. "Thank you."

"Don't mention it."

After seven trips, Heidi had everything she needed and set about arranging the food tables. She lit warming candles and put out serving spoons, watching as tenants began trickling in, a good twenty minutes before the scheduled event was to begin.

"They'd rather get here early than risk not getting here at all," Basile explained.

"Is that why you were at the door to help me?"

His cloudy blue eyes twinkled at her. "Oh, a sassy gal. I like 'em sassy."

"You like 'em any way they come," Mrs. Williams said, checking in. "No offense to you, Miss Joblowski."

"None taken." Heidi glanced around the room. "Who's the birthday boy?" she asked.

"You're speaking to him," Basile said.

Heidi stared at the older man as if she'd just come down with instant Alzheimer's. She looked at Mrs. Williams, who grinned and nodded.

"You're kidding?" she said. "You're a hundred?"

Basile looked at his watch. "Well, not yet, I'm not. I have another two hours and eleven minutes to go." He adjusted his grip on his walker. "But I'll accept any birthday kisses you'd like to give me now, if it's just the same to you. You never know what can happen in two hours and eleven minutes."

Heidi laughed and leaned closer, intending to give him a peck on the cheek. He turned at the last minute and she met his dry lips instead.

He grinned at her, as mischievous as any younger man she'd ever met. "Never underestimate a man's intentions."

"Oh, trust me," she said with humor. "I don't intend to again."

He chuckled. "Good. Because men can get away with a lot with a nice girl like you. Didn't your grandfather ever tell you that?" He wheeled his walker in the opposite direction. "Now if you'll excuse me, I'm going to see what other birthday kisses I can rustle up."

Mrs. Williams shook her head as she helped put out napkins and plates. "Keeps things lively, that one."

"I can imagine."

The other woman looked at her. "Trust me, you can't."

The lunch went swimmingly, with everyone enjoying the meal she'd prepared. The large cake was nearly history and laughter and conversation filled the room.

Heidi had had conversations with several of the residents and wished she'd been in a mindset to enjoy more. She hadn't had grandparents growing up and she liked interacting with the partygoers.

"Where's Basile?" Mrs. Williams asked.

Heidi was spooning the last of the baked beans into plastic containers. "I don't know. The last time I saw him was…" she tried to remember. "When he goosed Mrs. Benjamin and she laughed so hard she nearly lost her false teeth."

"At least fifteen minutes ago."

"Yes, probably about that."

The nurse sighed. "Here we go again."

"How do you mean?"

"I just noticed that Mrs. Jenkins is also missing."

"Bathroom breaks?"

"Together?"

Heidi squinted at her. "You're not saying…"

"That the birthday boy is trying to finnagle some birthday nookie?"

"No way! He's a hundred years old."

"And your point is?"

Heidi leaned closer to her. "I thought Basile was sweet on Mrs. Benjamin."

"He is. He targets the easy ones for these encounters. He'll have a nice visit with Mrs. Benjamin later when they listen to the latest James Patterson novel on CD."

Heidi held up her hand. "Too much information for this one girl to take in all at once."

"I'm not gossiping. I'm asking you to help me find them before they break something."

HEIDI WAS AFRAID the image of Basile getting birthday nookie from Mrs. Jenkins in the broom closet would forever be burned in the backs of her eyelids.

"The wonders of Viagra and KY," Mrs. Williams had muttered.

"Hey, where are you?" Nina asked Heidi.

"Hmm?" Heidi slowly tuned back in to the here and now. She'd long since closed up shop at the nursing home, returned home to clean up, stopped by BMC to make a batch of sweet dough for the morning rolls, and met up with her friends at the softball field. The bleachers were hard under her bottom, and the early evening was hot.

"I'm here—I hope," she finally answered Nina. "Trust me, I want to be anywhere but back at that nursing home right now."

Lindsay, one of the other players' girlfriends, gave an affected shiver on the opposite side of Nina. "Old people give me the creeps."

An older man in a ball cap turned around and sent her a dirty look.

Lindsay gave an eye roll. "I meant, one of the first

things I can ever remember is finding my grandfather dead. I was four and it wasn't pretty."

Heidi frowned. "Yeah, well today I got a bird's eye view of a one-hundred-year-old man sowing oats I would have thought he'd long run out of."

The man in front of them muttered something and moved farther down the bench.

Nina laughed and elbowed her. "Haven't you been around older people before? My grandparents used to disappear from the dining-room table at Thanksgiving and we'd hear them in the next room going at it gangbusters."

Heidi was familiar with Nina's grandmother Gladys and couldn't say she was surprised. Horror-struck, but not surprised. "What did you guys do?"

Nina shrugged. "Nothing. Just waited for them to come out and pretended we didn't see that her bra strap was sticking out of her collar or that his hair was mussed up."

"What are you doing?" Heidi asked Lindsay, who was staring intently at the field.

"Trying to imagine what Jack, or any of these guys for that matter, would be like at a hundred."

"Would you stop?"

Heidi followed her gaze, looking first at Kyle. She caught herself and refocused her attention on Jesse. She had a good idea what he'd look like at an older age because she knew his parents and he was the spitting image of his father. Hair grayer, lines a little deeper, a little thicker around the middle, but basically he'd be the same attractive, athletic guy.

She found her gaze sliding back to Kyle. Interestingly enough, she couldn't seem to bring herself to care what he would look like when he was older. She had the sensation that she'd feel the same way about him no matter how he aged.

"Do you think it's in our genes?" she said quietly.

"Is what in our genes?" Nina asked.

"That desire to sow our wild oats."

Nina leaned forward. "Are you talking about yourself—or Jesse? You don't think Jesse's messing around on you, do you?"

"Don't be ridiculous," Heidi said, and waved her friend away in case she started questioning her a little too closely.

Loud female hooting rose up from the bleachers of the visiting team and all three women looked over.

"Holy shit. Who's the Hooters girl?" Lindsay asked.

The tall, busty blonde could have easily qualified as one of the restaurant chain's waitresses. She wore a snug tank top that dipped deeply into her generous cleavage, and the low-slung shorts she wore were almost smaller than the panties Heidi had on under her own far more conservative capris.

"I haven't seen her before," Nina said. "How about you, Heidi?"

"Huh? Oh. No."

"Go, Jesse!" the woman shouted.

Nina turned to stare at Heidi.

"What? I said I didn't know who she was."

"Yes, well, if I were you," Lindsay said, "I'd want to find out. A girl like that…"

"A girl like that what?" Heidi prompted.

"A girl like that has a way of making most any man want to sow a few wild oats." Lindsay looked down at her own cleavage and gave her breasts a boost, then frowned. "Some girls have all the luck."

"Pay no attention to her," Nina said to Heidi. "Probably it's just someone Jesse knows from work."

"Probably."

But something about the way the woman had called out to Jesse made the hair on the back of Heidi's neck stand on end.

_12_

"WHAT HAPPENED to you? Did you get lost on the way from the ball field?"

Heidi slid into the booth next to Nina. The bar was filled to capacity, as it usually was on game day. "I had a couple of errands to run."

A lie to be sure. She hadn't had anything to do, but she wasn't going to own up to that.

Truth was, she was putting off coming face-to-face with Jesse. He'd conked out last night before she'd had a chance to talk to him, and she hadn't seen him since. She knew he expected her to be at the game, so she'd gone, but she'd exchanged only a wave with him and ignored a wave from Kyle.

So instead of going straight to the bar with everyone else after the game, she'd stopped in at home instead, pacing the floor and trying to decide what she was going to do. Her mind was now made up.

She had to stop this procrastinating and tell Jesse the truth.

"God, girl, what have you been doing?" Lindsay asked. "Were you and Jesse up all night having catch-up sex?"

"What?" Heidi practically croaked.

"You look like you haven't had a lick of sleep."

"Oh. That." Heidi gestured vaguely. "Been a rough couple of days, that's all."

Lindsey felt around in her purse. "Here. Use my concealer. The circles under your eyes are big enough to skip rocks on."

Nina gasped. "Lindsay!"

"What? They are. I should know. I've had them often enough myself. And this stuff," she waved the concealer. "Works miracles."

Too bad it didn't work on anything more than dark circles, Heidi thought. There were a couple of areas of her life she'd like to make disappear.

She took the makeup stick, grabbed her own purse and made her way toward the restrooms. Jesse had yet to spot her from the opposite side of the bar, where he was playing pool.

Unfortunately, Kyle had seen her and followed her to the hall that led to the johns.

"Not now," she said under her breath as she passed him.

"When then?"

"Never."

He put an arm across her path, stopping her. She took a deep breath. "Not an option."

"Well it's the only one available to you."

"Why?"

She squinted at him. He couldn't possibly be serious. "What do you mean why?"

"Exactly what you think it means."

"Kyle…"

He grinned at her. "What?"

"I'm telling Jesse."

KYLE HAD no other choice but to release his hold on her.

He stood back, not sure if he was relieved or disappointed that she didn't move.

"I think you should wait this out. At least until tomorrow."

She stared at him, her warm brown eyes looking huge. He guessed the slight smudges beneath them were caused by lack of sleep.

"Why?" she whispered.

A male customer exited the men's room and stopped in front of them, shrugging. Kyle moved to give him free passage.

"This thing has disaster written all over it," Heidi said.

"Does it? From where I stand, I don't think it does."

"That's because you don't have anything to lose."

"Don't I? Look, Jesse's my best friend. The only true friend I've ever had in my life. A life littered with foster family after foster family. My mother was a drug addict who died of an overdose six months after leaving me at the hospital and I'll never know my father because he was probably just another way for my mother to get a fix."

He cursed under his breath. Not even Jesse knew the truth of his upbringing. The families that wanted to keep him but couldn't because he never trusted them enough to let them in. The long nights spent working at fast-food joints and studying in the library when he was sixteen so he could live on his own and work toward a scholarship to Boston U. The way Jesse had come into his life at a time when he'd never expected to change his low opinion of human nature. Jesse had upended everything Kyle had ever believed about people raised differently from him simply by being his friend, then his best friend.

"I'd say I have a lot to lose, Heidi. A damn precious lot."

She searched his face and he let her, though it had to be one of the toughest things he'd ever done.

"Why would you risk it then?" she whispered, looking stunned and curious and all too sexy.

Why, indeed.

He looked over her shoulder at the oblivious crowd a few feet away in the bar.

"Come here…"

She gasped but didn't fight him when he steered her through the men's room door. With a hand on her arm, he looked around. Empty. He turned the lock on the door and then led her to an empty stall, guiding her in and closing the door behind him.

"What…what are you doing?" she asked.

He could tell she was fighting for indignation. Instead the quick flick of her tongue at the corner of her mouth betrayed her desire to do exactly what he wanted to do. And that was kiss her.

DEAR Lord, she'd turned into a ho.

The thought trailed through Heidi's mind as Kyle leaned into her inside the men's room stall and kissed her…and she kissed him back. Although back would be a relative turn, because, damn it, she wanted to devour him whole.

This wasn't supposed to be happening. Jesse was home, she was going to tell him what she and Kyle had done, and everything was supposed to go back to normal.

Yet here she was making out with Kyle in the men's

room…and she didn't care about anything but how she could possibly get closer to him.

She ran her fingers restlessly through his crisp hair, pulling him closer, tugging him back so she could feast on his neck. He smelled so good. He felt even better.

A small voice told her she shouldn't be doing this. That Jesse was in the other room and the chances of being caught were high. But she couldn't make herself care. If anything, the rush of knowing the risks made her even hotter for the man slipping his fingers under her shirt and reaching for her breasts, as hot for her as she was for him.

Dear God, what had she gotten herself into? Everywhere he touched, fire raged in its wake, robbing her of breath and making her hungrier yet. She kissed him again and again, hooking her right leg around his and pulling him closer yet, her other hand finding his tight bottom and squeezing him through his slacks. He smelled slightly sweaty from the game earlier and she licked the salt from his skin, the scent calling out to something elemental within her. Something wild.

Had she ever been so brazen with anyone else? Growing up, she'd always made sure she was above reproach, a role model for her younger sisters, forever trying to mold herself into the type of person she wanted to be.

But now…

Now the urgent voices within her refused to be quieted. Almost as if she'd locked her heart away, sentenced it to life in prison for fear of where it might lead her. And now it had grown so large that it had shattered the bars trying to hold it in place. It throbbed so forcibly, Heidi was afraid it might beat right through her ribcage.

But she'd loved Jesse. She knew a moment of pause as she drew back and took in Kyle's handsome features. It didn't escape her attention that she'd used the past tense in describing her feelings for Jesse.

But she did still love him, didn't she?

Then why was she making out with his best friend in the men's john?

None of this made any sense.

Kyle grasped her hips and kissed her again. She moaned. Screw it. Who wanted sense when she could have this right here, right now?

Kyle popped the front catch on her jeans and tugged down the zipper, then curved his fingers beneath the elastic of her panties. Heidi clutched his shoulders tightly, trembling from head to foot even as she cried out.

He kissed her, presumably to quiet her as much as to explore the depths of her mouth. She restlessly kissed him back, seeking the front of his jeans and hurriedly freeing him. She wanted him more than anything she'd ever wanted in her life.

Within seconds, but what seemed like agonizing minutes, she held the hot length of him in her palm.

Mmm…

She caressed the hard shaft for only a moment before he jerked out of her grasp.

"No," he whispered in her ear. "I don't have protection."

Heidi made a sound of frustration, having been left in the lurch one too many times lately.

Her eyes widened slightly. Where had this wild, demanding woman come from? While she'd always enjoyed what she considered to be a healthy sexual appetite, she'd never had a hose-him-down-and-bring-him-to-my-tent mentality.

But that's exactly what she felt now. She wanted release from the incredible pressure building in her stomach. And she wanted it *now.*

Kyle began tucking himself back into his jeans and she made a sound of protest. He was not going to stop what he had started without finishing, damn it.

He rested a finger against her lips and she made to bite the delectable flesh.

"Shh," he said. "Come here."

She accepted his kiss, mentally preparing herself for the cessation of his affection. No protection, no sex. Wasn't that the way it went?

He began to pull away and defeat settled in around her shoulders…until she realized he wasn't turning to leave. Rather he was lowering one knee to the floor even as he tugged the denim of her jeans down over her hips.

She gasped loudly, nearly climaxing right there on the spot.

She reached both hands out until they met with the stall walls and steadied herself.

Oh, yes!

13

"A CHANCE to be with you is worth the risk," he said. "Any risk."

She looked dubious.

"You…" he continued before she could hurry away. "You do something to me, Heidi. You fascinate me in a way no one else has done before. For me, you're the thunderbolt—the 'you just know' that you hear when you ask people how they knew they were in love." He cupped her chin in his palm. "You."

Kyle eyed the scrap of red silk barely covering her, the sight of women's underpants never failing to fascinate him. But that these particular panties belonged to Heidi made them doubly mesmerizing. Inches above the elastic top, her stomach quivered. He ran his fingers over the taut flesh there and then over to her hip, grasping her as he pressed his tongue against the dimple of her navel. He'd dreamed about kissing her, about touching her in such an intimate way for the past five days. And he feared that he'd never be able to do it again.

Now that he was doing it, he intended to draw the moment out for as long as he possibly could. Because he didn't know when, or if, he'd ever get the chance to again.

He swiped his thumbs over her hip bones and held her steady as he fastened his mouth over the front of her panties and blew hot air through the shiny fabric right onto her clit. She cried out and grasped his shoulders as if holding on for dear life.

With a quick tug, he freed her from her panties, helping her step from them as he had with her jeans. Standing there in her top and strappy sandals and nothing more, she looked like every guy's idea of a wet dream.

His idea of a wet dream come to life.

He positioned her so that her back was against the brick wall of the stall. She willingly went, permitting him full access. Kyle groaned as he took his visual fill of the bare, engorged flesh. So beautiful. So sensitive. He leaned forward and flicked his tongue along the length of her slit, reveling in the hot taste of her. He'd be damned if she didn't taste of lemons and honey. He pressed his fingers against her hips and she leaned against the wall, opening herself further to him. Her womanhood blossomed like a rare and beautiful flower and he took full advantage, fastening his lips around the tight bud and pulling the bit of flesh into his mouth.

"Oh, yes…oh, yes…"

Heidi's words only served to make him hotter. He curved his right hand around to her bottom, coaxing her to slide her leg to lie over his shoulder. She rested against the wall as he laved her, stroking her with his tongue even as he reached for her other leg, curving that one over his other shoulder.

Heidi joined her ankles behind his neck even as she grasped his shoulders for support.

Kyle worked the fingers of one hand up her inner

The Harlequin Reader Service — Here's how it works:

Accepting your 2 free books and 2 free mystery gifts places you under no obligation to buy anything. You may keep the books and gifts and return the shipping statement marked "cancel". If you do not cancel, about a month later we'll send you 6 additional books and bill you just $4.24 each in the U.S. or $4.71 each in Canada. That is a savings of at least 15% off the cover price. It's quite a bargain! Shipping and handling is just 25¢ per book, along with any applicable taxes.* You may cancel at any time, but if you choose to continue, every month we'll send you 6 more books, which you may either purchase at the discount price or return to us and cancel your subscription.

*Terms and prices subject to change without notice. Sales tax applicable in N.Y. Canadian residents will be charged applicable provincial taxes and GST. Offer not valid in Quebec. All orders subject to approval. Credit or debit balances in a customer's account(s) may be offset by any other outstanding balance owed by or to the customer. Please allow 4 to 6 weeks for delivery. Offer available while quantities last.

NO POSTAGE
NECESSARY
IF MAILED
IN THE
UNITED STATES

BUSINESS REPLY MAIL
FIRST-CLASS MAIL   PERMIT NO. 717   BUFFALO, NY

POSTAGE WILL BE PAID BY ADDRESSEE

HARLEQUIN READER SERVICE
3010 WALDEN AVE
PO BOX 1867
BUFFALO NY 14240-9952

If offer card is missing write to: The Harlequin Reader Service, 3010 Walden Ave., P.O. Box 1867, Buffalo, NY 14240-1867

Do You Have the LUCKY KEY?

PLAY THE
Lucky Key Game

and you can get

FREE BOOKS
and **FREE GIFTS!**

Scratch the gold areas with a coin. Then check below to see the books and gifts you can get!

YES! I have scratched off the gold areas. Please send me the 2 FREE BOOKS and 2 FREE GIFTS, worth about $10, for which I qualify. I understand I am under no obligation to purchase any books, as explained on the back of this card.

351 HDL EVLT   151 HDL EVP5

FIRST NAME   LAST NAME

ADDRESS

APT.#   CITY

STATE/ PROV.   ZIP/ POSTAL CODE

www.eHarlequin.com

2 free books plus 2 free gifts   1 free book

2 free books   Try Again!

DETACH AND MAIL CARD TODAY!

(H-B-11/08)

© 2008 HARLEQUIN ENTERPRISES LIMITED ® and ™ are trademarks owned and used by the trademark owner and/or its licensee.

thigh, pressing his thumb against her soaking portal as he reached his other hand up under her shirt, hooking her bra cup and lifting it until the pink nipple of her left breast popped out.

Oh, what a wonderfully erotic picture she made, this spectacularly sexy woman who was not afraid to bare herself to him, fully and unconditionally. He'd seen a glimpse of her in the café kitchen, but this…the sight of her was enough to send him into a heightened sense of awareness that he'd never experienced before. And feared he might never again.

He moved so both his hands cupped her perfect bottom, joining his thumbs together in front of her vagina even as he licked her.

There was the sound of someone at the door. Kyle stilled his actions, but held an alert Heidi firmly in place.

"Hey! Is somebody in there?"

Kyle was afraid their unwelcome visitor would yank Heidi out of the gauzy cloud of sensation he'd worked so hard to place her in. He closed his eyes and offered up a small prayer.

A prayer that was answered when the guy left.

Heidi made a move to free herself.

Kyle refused her the easy exit.

"Shhh," he said softly.

He purposefully suckled her clit again, quickly entering her with both thumbs at the same time.

She instantly tensed up at the unexpected action, her breath coming in shallow gasps, the distraction instantly forgotten. Her head moved restlessly against the wall even as she watched him through heavy-lidded eyes, as if she couldn't take her gaze from him if she tried.

Kyle replaced his thumbs with his middle finger, then his middle and index finger, thrusting them into her slick flesh, twisting them and then pulling them out again…then again. When he judged her ready, he fastened his lips over her bud again and sucked deeply, pushing her effectively over the edge.

HEIDI DISSOLVED into a series of uncontrollable spasms, taken to the ultimate height of sensation. She wouldn't have cared who walked through the door at that moment. Nothing would have stopped her from experiencing this very moment. This exquisite sensation of floating upward to a place so breathtakingly beautiful that she never wanted to leave.

But, of course, she had to leave. Life on this faraway planet was unsustainable for more than a few, precious moments. Which was exactly what made it so very special.

She collapsed against the wall, little more than a boneless rag doll as Kyle coaxed out a few aftershocks. His movements were maddenly thorough as he lapped her clean.

She swallowed hard. She hadn't known such sensations existed. Oh, she'd reached climax before. But what Kyle had just given her far surpassed anything she'd ever experienced.

Kyle shifted her until her feet were once again on the floor, relatively speaking, and licked his way up her abdomen, taking her bared nipple into his mouth and pulling deeply. Heat accumulated in her belly anew as she entwined her fingers in his hair. Then she drew him up so she could kiss him, tasting her own musk on his tongue.

Before she knew it, she was in a state of urgent need all over again. She wanted more than his fingers and mouth. She wanted him.

"You're killing me here, Heidi," he whispered against her mouth.

"Tell me about it."

She ran her hands restlessly all over his body, fighting his protests when she undid his fly and freed his throbbing erection. Her mouth watered at the prospect of tasting his salty flesh against her tongue. But he refused her access, turning her instead to face the wall.

"But we don't have protection," she weakly protested, running her tongue over her parched lips even as she anticipated him telling her to hell with a condom, he needed to feel her around him no matter the consequences. And, lord forgive her, she wanted the same.

"For what I have in mind, we won't need it."

She'd practiced the withdrawal method before, when she was much younger. Until she'd been shocked by how lucky she'd been not to become pregnant. From there on in she'd insisted on protection.

But now…

She gasped when she felt Kyle's fingers slide between her thighs from behind, slightly parting her legs. She arched her back, giving him greater access. She knew a fear that she might spontaneously combust. She wanted him. Fully. Now.

Kyle's fingers fluttered against her clit and then her vagina, finding her wet and willing. Heidi couldn't seem to catch her breath. She pressed her cheek and now bared breasts against the cool brick, seeking gravity. She didn't find it as Kyle positioned his hot, hard shaft so that it rested between her thighs and then grasped her hips until her flesh covered him.

"Sweet Jesus…"

His words reflected the chaotic sensations rolling through her.

Heidi knew an immediate desire to buck her hips so that he might enter her, but sucked her bottom lip between her teeth to quell the desire, instead forcing herself to wait and see what he might do.

Kyle slid his erection back between the slick valley of her swollen labia, then forward again, the tip diving up briefly to bump her tight bud. She gasped, a need welling up in her to have him deep inside her.

He rhythmically stroked her with his hard, long length and she rewarded him with liquid proof of her approval, amazed that she could derive so much pleasure from such a simple act.

Kyle grasped her hips, bending her forward as far as she could go in the cramped environs. Then he held her still.

Heidi held her breath. He wasn't…he couldn't be about to…

He gently fit his head against her portal. She shivered in sweet anticipation of his breach. He entered her mere millimeters, stretching her muscles and giving her but a taste of what she so desired.

He entered her again and she tried to bear back against him, force him deeper, but he held her fast, only going in a little farther than the time before.

Then he let rip a muffled curse and pulled out, sand-wiching himself between her engorged flesh again and stroking her, creating a friction that threatened to consume her in flames.

He stiffened and Heidi instantly climaxed at the demonstration of his desire for her. She wrapped her fingers around the thick staff and drew up and down, helping him find his way to ecstasy.

Long moments later they clung together, breathless and sweaty…but nowhere near satisfied.

"This isn't going to do it for me," Kyle whispered into her ear, holding her close.

Heidi felt his hard-on against her hip. "Me neither. More. I want more."

He placed his hands on either side of her head and kissed her lingeringly, gazing deep into her eyes.

"My place," he said hoarsely. "I don't care when. In an hour. The middle of the night. I'll be there. Waiting."

Anticipation built within her. "Okay."

14

WITH THE HELP of Kyle, Heidi made a quick exit and hurried to the ladies' room, sitting for long moments in an empty stall to compose herself. She hadn't begun to feel guilty yet, though she knew that would soon come.

She rested her head in her hands and closed her eyes, her body still humming with need for a man she had no right to.

Was it possible to want one man with your head, and another with your body?

A week ago, she'd have answered an unequivocal no. And since she was completely devoted to Jesse, she would have gone on to give anyone who asked an earful of how happy she was in her relationship and that Jesse gave her everything she ever needed.

Then came Kyle...

Literally.

She squeezed her eyes tighter along with her thighs, shivering as she recalled their hot, decadent moments together just minutes before.

Jesse...

Her throat tightened as she quickly got up, refusing to think about anything just then but the need to get to Kyle's place as soon as possible.

She knew where his house was. Had never been inside, but had dropped Jesse off a couple times, or picked him up. It was a modern design in the northern part of town. It wasn't in a subdivision, although it certainly would have fitted right in. Kyle had chosen instead a single, acre-large parcel of land and set his house in the middle of it, careful to maintain much of the original forest that had long since been cleared for surrounding developments.

In front of the sink, she smiled at another woman and went about splashing her face with cold water and then reapplying makeup both to cover the dark circles under her eyes, and to erase any evidence of her recent activities. Her hair was a tangled mess and it took a good five minutes to tame it.

She inhaled several deep breaths and tried to come up with an excuse to leave her group of friends.

The door opened. "Hey," Lindsay said, joining her at the sinks. "Are you all right?"

Heidi nearly croaked. "All right? Why wouldn't I be all right?"

Lindsay squinted at her in the mirror. "It's taking you a long time to put on that concealer. And you look a little clammy." She pressed the back of her hand against Heidi's forehead. "You're running a fever."

Oh, she was ill, all right. Just not in the way Lindsay thought.

Then it occurred to Heidi. Her excuse out of there.

"Actually, I'm not feeling very well. I think it might have been something I ate earlier."

"Your own food?"

Heidi smiled. The chef made sick from her own cooking.

Then again, the scenario didn't far miss the mark. Her current situation was directly related to her own behavior. No one had forced her into Kyle's arms. He hadn't seduced her. If anything, she'd unexpectedly seduced him. So she had no one to blame but herself.

"Maybe you should go home," Lindsay suggested. "Make yourself some of that great chicken soup of yours and rest."

Heidi considered exactly what she planned to do when she left and it had nothing to do with chicken soup or rest. "Yeah," she said. "Maybe I will do that."

She led the way out of the restroom, asking Lindsay to make her excuses to everyone, including Jesse, and ran straight into the busty blonde who had been cheering up a storm from the neighboring bleachers.

"Oh!" she said. "I'm sorry. I didn't see you."

"My bad," the other woman said. "I wasn't watching where I was going."

"No problem." Heidi was the last person to hold anyone responsible for not paying attention. Her mind was on a few other things as well.

The woman continued toward the restroom.

"Fake," Lindsay said.

"What?"

"Her boobs. Fake. Gotta be. No one with breasts that big can go without a bra unless they're fake."

"Yes, well, they're hers whether she was born with them or paid for them."

KYLE STOOD at the bar in shock.

After leaving Heidi in the ladies' room, he'd made his way out to join the cast of dozens and stood at the bar to get a fresh beer. He'd already had a bottle with the guys back at the pool tables, but he figured he could use all the extra time he could buy before going back to make his apologies to the group and leave. His only thought was to get back to his place as soon as humanly possible.

He accepted the cold bottle and rested it against his temple. Guilt gremlins threatened from every side, nipping at his conscience and making him feel like the heel he knew himself to be.

He turned and ran into the very last person he'd expected to see there: Mona Malone.

He'd figured it was a figment of his imagination when he thought he'd spotted her at the ballpark, easily dismissing it as a case of mistaken identity.

His gaze immediately sought Jesse.

"Kyle!" the bleached blonde exclaimed as if they were long-lost friends. *Long* and *lost* might have fitted, because the last time he'd seen her he'd been living in Boston. But *friend* far from made the cut.

He stood ramrod-straight as she threw her arms around him and gave him a loud kiss on the cheek, gaining the attention of nearly every healthy male in the place with her short shorts and tight tank top. Which, he had no doubt, was exactly her intention.

"Mona," he said coolly. "Imagine meeting you here." He took a long pull from his beer to force her to step away. "Wait. Don't tell me. You were in the neighborhood and decided to stop in?"

"No, silly! After hearing you guys brag about how great this little town of yours was, I just had to check it out."

Finally Kyle spotted Jesse coming up behind Mona.

"Excuse me," Kyle said to Mona, not caring how rude he was being.

He grabbed Jesse's arm and led him a few feet away.

"What in the hell do you think you're doing?" Kyle asked under his breath.

"Why do you presume I'm immediately to blame?" Jesse asked. "Hey, I didn't know she was coming here."

Kyle narrowed his gaze.

Jesse looked down and then away. He paled and Kyle saw why. He'd just spotted Heidi making her way back from the restrooms with Lindsay.

"I've got to go to the little girl's room," Mona announced.

Kyle started toward her. Jesse stopped him midway, this time taking his arm and leading him away.

"Hey, man, I've got a big favor to ask you…"

Kyle tensed. He remembered Jesse's favors. He'd done enough of them while they were away at college together.

"What kind of favor?"

"A big favor. Huge. Gigantic."

Kyle watched over his shoulder as Mona literally bumped into Heidi. And if he was any expert on human behavior, he suspected Mona knew who Heidi was and had done it on purpose.

Jesse cursed under his breath. "I need you to act like you and Mona…"

Mona split from the two women and continued on toward the washrooms, avoiding what he'd feared would be a scene.

"What!" he asked, returning his attention to his friend. "Oh, no." He held his hands up, gripping his beer bottle in one. "I might have done a lot of things for you in Boston, but not here. You're on your own now, buddy."

The thought of presenting himself as being or ever having been involved with the oversexed and under-dressed Mona Malone gave him the creeps. But the idea of doing it in front of Heidi made him feel fully sick.

"Come on, Ky. You're not seeing anyone. Who's to say Mona isn't just some girl you used to know? Heidi…"

He ran his hand through his hair several times in an agitated state unlike any Kyle had ever seen him in.

Kyle pulled his friend's hand down so no one else would notice the guilty giveaways. "Just chill, bro."

Jesse was shaking his head now. "I can't let Heidi find out, man. It would break her heart if she knew that Mona and I had been a couple all through college."

"Yes, well, you should have thought about that before you did it."

Jesse stared at him. "There was no reason to think I had anything to worry about. Mona was in Boston. Heidi was here. And never the twain shall meet and all that."

"Don't bring Kipling anywhere near this fiasco."

"Come on, Kyle. It's been a long time since I've asked you for anything, man. Do this one thing for me. Just for tonight. By tomorrow, I swear, Mona will be on her way back home and no one need be any the wiser."

Kyle drew in a deep breath and looked around. He half hoped someone else would enter the fray and take the unwanted load he carried from his shoulders.

It had been a long time since he'd thought about

their years as college roommates. But the events unraveling around him reminded him all too much of the past.

How many times had he answered the phone when they were roommates in Boston and lied to Heidi while Jesse had been otherwise engaged? How many times had he made excuses for his friend? How many times had he spent longer talking to Heidi than her own supposed boyfriend?

He realized that was when he'd fallen for the pretty girl in the photograph next to Jesse's bed. During phone calls meant for Jesse, she'd shared what she was going through at home and school while Kyle listened. He'd barely said anything. He hadn't had to. Most of their conversations would end with her clearing her throat and apologizing for talking his ear off. And, oh, could he tell Jesse she'd called?

It wasn't until recently that he'd learned she'd believed his lack of participation in their conversations, and his reluctance to interact with her in general, was a result of his dislike of her.

Rather it had been his intense like.

Jesse clapped his hand on Kyle's shoulder, returning him solidly to a present that resembled the past a little too closely. Except for one thing. Heidi was no longer a faraway voice on the phone. She was a flesh-and-blood woman who was threatening to make off with his heart.

"Come on, Ky. Please? I promise, this is the last time I'll ever ask you to cover for me."

His friend was in such a pitiful state, Kyle didn't know whether to slug him or hug him. Especially considering that just a few short minutes ago he had been taking liberties with Jesse's girlfriend, and his friend was none the wiser.

Suddenly, his head hurt.

He didn't know what to say, so he said nothing. And the decision was taken out of his hands when Heidi and Lindsay joined them…and a split second later Mona did, as well.

"Hey, baby," Mona said, snaking her arm over Kyle's shoulders. "Aren't you going to introduce me to your friends?"

The obvious lead-in set his teeth on edge. Apparently she and Jesse had already discussed throwing him in as the decoy. Which meant that his friend had known about Mona's presence in the city longer than just five minutes ago.

He was going to kill Jesse.

Of course, in order to do that, he'd have to survive his friend's wrath when Jesse found out about him and Heidi.

He needed to get out of there, but quick. And he had no intention of doing it with Mona in tow.

Jesse made the introductions. "Mona here and Kyle go way back," he was saying, nodding like a bobble-head. "To Boston, actually." He chuckled. "You couldn't have parted the two of them with a crowbar."

Kyle could have done without the embellishments.

He looked at Heidi to find her skin pale and her eyes wide. There was no doubt she was both surprised… and hurt.

And he damned Jesse all over again for his selfishness.

And cursed himself for his runaway hormones and stupidity.

15

"SHE DOESN'T LOOK like his type, somehow," Nina ventured aloud.

Heidi took a batch of sweet rolls from the oven in the café kitchen, nearly burning her hand as she transferred the tray to the island counter to cool.

"Damn." She shook her hand and stared at the red stripe on the side of her finger.

"Let me see."

She allowed Nina to play mother hen.

"Cold water should take care of it." She led Heidi to the sink and turned on the water, holding her hand under the spray. The cold dulled the burning.

"Thanks," Heidi said quietly.

"Don't mention it." Nina handed her a towel and then leaned against the sink, crossing her arms over her chest. "Are you all right? You don't look so good."

Heidi nodded. "I'm fine."

She just hadn't had two hours of sleep in the past two days, that's all. And if things continued as they were, she was afraid she might never sleep again.

"Kevin thinks something fishy's going on," Nina said.

"Huh?" Heidi looked at her. "Fishy? With me?"

Nina smiled and moved the tray from the island to the cooling rack. "No, not you. With this Mona girl."

If she heard that name one more time, Heidi's head was going to explode.

"Look, I'm not really up for gossip this morning," she said. "You know, if it's all the same to you."

Nina shrugged. "No skin off my back. I just thought you might know more about the woman and where she comes from."

"Never heard of her before and I haven't a clue."

It was just after 6:00 a.m. and they would be opening the doors in a half hour for the early risers looking for a cup of steaming hot coffee and a roll to go. Most everything was prepared, or on its way to being ready, so Heidi moved on to the other tasks she'd planned to do that morning. She needed to make fresh onion buns for Jesse's surprise birthday party, along with cookies and the cake itself. She figured since she would already be making the buns for the café's lunch hour, she'd get the chore out of the way. After lunch, she'd make the little wrapped wieners everyone always seemed to like so much, as well as the feta-cheese pies, then store both in the freezer until the morning of the party. For some reason she couldn't fathom, both baked better after some time in the freezer.

"Kevin thinks she's from Boston," Nina said.

Heidi stared at her. "Probably, seeing that's where Kyle's from."

She really didn't want to talk about this. Just remembering the way the sexy blonde had hung on to Kyle's arm last night at the bar made her chest ache in an unfamiliar way.

One minute she and Kyle had been going at it hot and heavy in a men's-room stall, the next a woman she'd hardly even known existed was kissing his neck in public. Doing exactly what she wanted to be doing that minute.

She knew she should have left. Should have made her excuses and gone home, saved herself from the misery of watching Mona stamp her claim all over Kyle. But she had been rooted to the spot, incapable of taking her gaze from them…and helpless to stop herself from hurting so deeply.

She slapped a length of risen dough onto the counter and madly punched it down.

Thankfully Jesse hadn't seemed to notice anything amiss. But she hadn't really thought about that until later while she was lying, alone, in bed. She'd been so consumed with the idea that Kyle had a girlfriend and had never said anything to her about it that she hadn't thought about anything else.

Of course, she and Kyle really didn't seem to do much talking when they had the chance. At least not about things that had anything to do with their pasts.

She flattened the dough with long, even strokes of the rolling pin, barely aware of Nina making soup in the corner.

Ever since she was a young girl, Heidi had loved baking and cooking. There existed a rhythm in the simple, often repetitive actions in which she found a sense of peace. Usually.

Now, that familiar rhythm gave her too much time to think.

Perhaps Mona's appearance was fate's way of solving

one of her dilemmas. It seemed more than a coincidence that the woman had appeared right before she'd been preparing to go to Kyle's place and complicate the situation even more than it already was.

Agitated, she swiped at her forehead with the back of her hand and considered the dough she'd just rolled out.

"Okay, that's it," Nina said, swiveling her toward the sink to wash her hands again. "You're officially banned from the kitchen."

KYLE SAT at the counter of the café, trying to catch a glimpse of Heidi through the small window in the door. So far, he hadn't had any luck. He'd seen her car in the lot, so he knew she was working today.

Had she spotted him and was hiding?

He grimaced as he pretended an interest in the simple menu in his hands, the idea of her avoiding him doing strange things to his psyche.

He wouldn't say he was a man used to getting what he wanted. But he could say that he wasn't used to wanting what he couldn't have. Interesting since he'd wanted Heidi the day he'd first laid eyes on her eight months ago. He'd been impressed with the way he'd managed his runaway lust…up until he'd succumbed to it. Since then, he felt like little more than a hormone-ridden teen looking for ways to be in the same place as his friend's girl just so he could catch a glimpse of her.

"Can I help you?"

Kyle looked at the teenager on the other side of the counter. "What I wouldn't give if you could help me."

She gave him a puzzled expression. "Why don't I let you have a few more minutes to decide?"

It was going to take far more than a few minutes to decide anything in his life right now, unfortunately.

"Kyle…"

Heidi's voice.

Strangely, every tense muscle in his body uncoiled at the soft, familiar sound.

He put the menu aside and smiled up at her. She'd just exited the kitchen and was holding a tray of fresh baked rolls, apparently en route to the display case.

For an excruciating moment, the world seemed to move in slow motion, everyone going about their business while he and Heidi gazed at each other.

Then, suddenly, the world righted itself and returned to real time.

Heidi put the tray down on the counter in front of him, whispering, "What are you doing here?"

He pretended an interest in the rolls. "Having lunch, of course."

"There are at least a dozen other places in a three-block radius where you could have eaten. Why'd you come here?"

"Isn't that obvious?"

Heidi stared at him and then her shoulders appeared to relax. And she smiled, melting every shred of uncertainty within him.

Yes, it was obvious, he thought. His being drawn to her. It didn't matter where he went, what he did—all he could think about was being close to her.

"Everything's changed," Heidi said simply.

Kyle nodded. "I know. I was there last night, remember?"

"I know."

That same pained expression he'd glimpsed yesterday shadowed her face and he silently cursed the day that Jesse was even born.

"How's Mona?" she asked.

He wanted to ask how in the hell he was supposed to know, but stopped himself.

Instead, he said, "Fine, I guess. I haven't seen her since last night."

The answer didn't improve Heidi's expression. If anything, it worsened it.

"We said goodnight at the bar," he clarified, realizing his vague statement left room for her to think he'd slept with Mona. "How about Jesse?"

"What about him?"

He didn't say anything.

"I haven't seen him since we were all together at the bar."

"I meant have you spoken to him…?"

He intentionally let the question dangle.

She avoided his gaze as she picked up the tray and moved toward the display case a couple of feet away. "No. Not yet."

"But…?"

She hadn't said the word, but he sensed it was on the tip of her tongue.

But everything would go back to normal now that Jesse was back? That she would miraculously stop wanting Kyle? That he would incredibly stop wanting her?

"But I will."

"There's another game tonight."

Her eyes clouded over briefly. She must have forgotten about the softball game.

What had she thought would happen tonight? Did she plan to jump back into her relationship with Jesse feet first and hope that she could repair everything?

"We need to talk," he said firmly.

Heidi gave him a knowing, suspicious look. "We've talked enough."

She turned and slid the empty tray into a large trolley and began wheeling it toward the kitchen.

"Heidi?"

She stopped, but didn't turn to face him.

"We haven't spoken nearly enough."

He got up to leave, glancing over his shoulder to find her staring after him with a mixture of fear, pain and longing.

HEIDI SAT in her car outside her mother's house, wishing there were at least a tree around to shield her from the unrelenting heat of the sun. She had air conditioning, but Jesse had told her earlier in the summer that she needed to get a fresh canister of ozone, or freon, or something like that. At any rate, she hadn't had a chance to get around to it yet with everything going on.

She leaned forward to see if she could spot her mother, then lay on the horn again. Instead, she saw a round face pop up in the lower half of the screen door, and a tiny, fisted hand banging against the screen. Her sister's son, Tyler. He was mouthing something. Heidi turned down the radio and cracked open the window from where she sat waiting at the curb fifteen feet away.

"It's a sunny…sunny day…" the three-year-old was saying.

"Hey, Tyler," she called out. "How are you doing, kiddo?"

He stopped and looked at her. Of course, odds were good he wouldn't recognize her. She didn't visit as often as she'd like.

She swallowed hard. What was she talking about? She went out of her way to make excuses not to visit.

Melody appeared and swept up little Tyler, then they both gave a wave and disappeared inside the house.

Heidi faced forward and briefly closed her eyes, battling off the guilt she seemed to be experiencing so often lately. An emotion she was used to feeling.

The passenger door opened and her mother climbed in.

"Woowee, girl, turn up the air conditioner already."

Heidi took in her mother's casual attire of jeans, sleeveless blouse and sandals, then edged her hand away from the control panel. "It doesn't go up any higher."

"Sounds like my car." Alice reached for her seatbelt as Heidi put the car in gear and drove away from the curb. "Speaking of crappy cars, thanks for offering to drive me to my appointment today. I don't know what's going on with the clunker, but Sandy thinks it might be the alternator because all I'm getting is this clicking sound when I turn the key."

"Sandy?"

"Yeah, you remember. The kid two streets up the block? You two went to school together. Anyway, he's a mechanic. Like his old man."

Heidi had completely forgotten about Sandy.

"Maybe it's the battery?" she suggested.

Alice shook her head. "No. There wouldn't be any sound if it were the battery." She sighed and settled against the seat more comfortably as if adjusting to the fact that it wasn't going to get any cooler. "Anyway, thanks for offering to pick me up."

Heidi hadn't offered. She'd been arm-twisted into seeing to a chore she would have gladly left to her sister, who, unfortunately, was also minus a car for the day because her good-for-nothing boyfriend and father of her child was using it to go see about a job in Taylor.

So she'd been called in to rescue her mother.

"Is everything all right, Heidi?"

Brows drawn together, she took her gaze from the road to stare at her mother. "What?"

"You look a little tired. Are you not getting enough rest?"

Heidi took a deep breath. "What do you know about me?"

"Pardon me?"

"I said, what do you know about me?"

Alice smiled. "I know more than you think I know."

"Oh, yeah? Tell me one thing. Just one thing. Because I don't think you know me at all."

"I know you're fond of taking mice and making them into elephants."

"Everybody does that."

"Maybe. But never as thoroughly as you. Stop sign."

"What?"

"I said, stop sign. Stop the car. Now."

Heidi realized she was five feet away from running straight through a two-way stop on a busy intersection. She jammed on the brakes just in time, although the nose of her car jutted beyond the crosswalk and she earned a few strident horn honks.

"Pull over, Heidi. It's time you and I had this out."

What was it with everybody thinking she needed to talk?

But as she looked at her mother, her forty-two-year-old pregnant mother, she knew that in this case, Alice was right…

16

"WHAT ABOUT your doctor's appointment?" Heidi asked, her knuckles white against the steering wheel.

"I'll reschedule. Now, pull over. I've been waiting for the opportunity for this conversation for a long time and I'm not about to let it pass us by."

Us. The word seemed so strange to Heidi somehow. It had been a long, long time since she'd thought of her mother and her in any shared context. There had always been Alice. And Heidi. And her sisters. But she couldn't remember a time when there had ever been a solid *us* in any capacity.

She chose a small roadside park that boasted a fenced-off children's playground, a small banquet hall and a covered picnic area. It was past lunchtime, so no one was picnicking. And there were only a few small children playing, their mothers watching nearby from under the shady trees. Heidi pulled in next to a picnic table and shut off the car. Alice rolled down her window.

After a long moment, she said, "So, tell me, little girl, what bug crawled up your ass and died?"

Heidi stared at the one person who had always been a fixture in her life, mostly unwanted, and reached to roll down her own window, the heat already filling the small car despite the shade of a nearby oak.

"First of all, don't call me 'girl.' I haven't been little, or a girl, for a very long time."

"Then stop acting like one."

Heidi opened her mouth to respond then snapped it shut.

"What? You expected I was just going to sit here and let you vent without a response?"

"I thought it might make for a refreshing change."

Alice mulled that over and then shifted so that she was facing Heidi. "Okay, then. Have at it."

Heidi felt every issue she'd ever had with her mother bubble up to the surface in that one moment. She followed her mother's lead and turned to face her more fully. "Why did you have me?"

She blinked. "What?"

"You heard me. Why did you ever have me? Or Melody? Or any of us girls?" She held up her fingers and began ticking off reasons why Alice should never have had any children. "First, you aren't, and have never been, in a financial position to support any of us adequately. And, excuse me, do you see any fathers around? Someone to help provide a stable family environment?"

She noticed the way her mother's hands went to her still-flat stomach and the new baby growing within her and felt a pinprick of guilt.

"Secondly, do you know what I went through as a kid? I was raised wearing secondhand clothes, sent to beg the school to qualify for the free lunch program because there was never anything to eat in the house. Do you know what that does to a kid? I was teased, I always felt like an outsider, like I wasn't deserving enough, or good enough, and would never fit in. I got my first paper route at ten just so I could buy a few school supplies that didn't come from the dollar store."

Alice flinched. But Heidi couldn't bring herself to care. She was too far gone. Too raw.

Her mother was right. This conversation had been a long time in coming. And she intended to purge herself of every last painful memory she had in her.

"Thirdly, what kind of role model do you think you make? Aside from me and Faith," she named her youngest sister, "three of your daughters have had babies of their own before they were twenty, out of wedlock, and don't have two nickels to rub together between them."

A mother walked by with her young son. Heidi watched as she put him in the back of a late-model Jeep and then drove away.

"God, I go out of my way to not visit your house because I hate being reminded of how I was raised. Hate remembering what it was like to always feel like the outsider looking in. Like the poor kids on the block because our mother never cared for anything but her own selfish needs."

Alice looked as if she'd been slapped. And for all intents and purposes, that's what Heidi had done.

She slumped against her own seat, drained by both the summer heat and the list of grievances, fair and unfair, that she'd been holding in for far too long. A lifetime's worth.

Neither of them said anything for long, tense moments.

Heidi concentrated on her breathing. In. Out. In. Her mind was a blank. She'd said what she'd wanted to say.

The question was, where did they go from here?

"Wow. That was much worse than I imagined it would be," her mother said quietly.

Heidi didn't say anything. Merely sat staring ahead of her as the leaves of the oak tree rustled in a light breeze, bringing the smell of freshly cut grass to her nose.

Alice said, "I knew this was coming. For a long time. Probably from the day you were born and looked up at me with those large, dark, questioning eyes." A softness had entered her voice that Heidi didn't want to acknowledge. "Even then you seemed to ask, 'So, you brought me here. Now what are you going to do with me'?"

Her mother laughed gently. "I always thought it was my own imagination. Being a first-time mother, I had no idea what to do. But I learned. We learned together." She cleared her throat. "Sure, there were mistakes. But, I'm sorry to tell you, none of them were the ones you just mentioned."

Heidi finally looked at her.

Alice wore a sad yet affectionate expression. "I always had this feeling that when it came to you, I'd forever come up wanting. Nothing would ever be good enough to please you. You were a bossy little thing, ordering your sisters around like a little commander, convinced that there wasn't anything out there you couldn't control or bend to your will."

Alice shook her head. "I kept waiting for life to teach you that you couldn't control everything. For you to learn that sometimes power lies in the surrendering of control. But it never came. Instead you used your own failings to further bolster your need for control. And every time you did, I fell down a few ladder steps in your eyes. It didn't matter what I did or didn't do, I was always the one to blame for life's shortcomings and disappointments."

She was quiet for a minute or two, then said so softly Heidi nearly didn't hear her, "Don't you think I wish that my life had turned out differently? That I had met and fallen in love with and married the one man meant for me? Do you think I planned to get pregnant with you while I was in college?

"But I won't apologize for it. I've always struggled to make sure all you girls had everything you needed. The house might not have been big, but it was always clean. And you all were clothed…maybe not in the designer things you wanted, but there was never any reason to be ashamed of yourself. And there was always food in the house. Just not the food that you thought there should be. Like the stuff in the pantries of your friends. You wanted macaroni and cheese out of that stupid box. I made fresh. You wanted all that junk food. I wouldn't have it."

Her mother turned toward her again. "At one time I actually hoped that you'd credit me for your interest in baking. I mean, who do you think put the raw ingredients in the cupboards? Who made sure there was always flour, baking powder and soda? Vanilla, which was expensive, and yeast? But you never seemed to realize that. Instead you credit your own survival techniques when, if you think about it, there was always food on the table.

"You kids never wanted for anything. I'll be the first to admit that we didn't have all the extras. But we did and still do have one thing that a lot of other families don't have—we have love. And each other. And that's always been enough for me."

Her voice caught and Heidi purposefully turned her head away, staring out her window and willing the breeze to dry any dampness collecting in her eyes. She remembered rainy days when she and her sisters and mother huddled under a blanket on the couch next to the front windows with big mugs of hot chocolate. And hot summer days when they'd stretched out side by side on towels spread on top of the grass in the backyard, sunning themselves as oldies played on the radio. And Christmas Eves when she would help her mother get ready for the next morning, all of them talking. Always talking. Sometimes singing. And laughing.

She'd forgotten about the laughter.

And the love.

"I'm sorry it wasn't enough for you, Heidi. Because we've missed you."

She realized that she'd missed them, too. And the comprehension was nearly her undoing.

Long minutes passed with neither of them saying anything. With Alice apparently out of words. With Heidi not knowing what to say.

Then her mother said, "I was raised to believe that what you got out of life was equal to what you put into it. I don't know. Maybe you're right. Maybe I didn't give you nearly enough of what you needed. And now I deserve to get nothing in return...

"But you…what can you honestly say you've put into life lately that didn't end up in a direct, quantifiable return for yourself, Heidi? And what value do you give love? Nothing?"

Heidi's heart contracted, resulting in a pain for which she was ill-prepared. The picture her mother painted was not only unflattering, it was selfish. *Was* she selfish? Had she expected much and given little?

She bit on her bottom lip so hard she nearly drew blood.

Alice appeared to be expecting her to say something. She said nothing, afraid that one word would be enough to open the floodgates she'd spent so much of her life leaning against to keep closed.

"Is that it?" her mother asked. "All this time you've been ashamed? Of me? Of your family?

"Take me home, Heidi. Now, please."

FOR A LONG TIME after Heidi dropped her mother back home, she kept driving around, not really seeing anything, concentrating on nothing more than the road ahead and her own conflicting emotions.

She was somewhat surprised to find herself sitting outside the nursing home. Sure, she'd left a couple of trays there with leftovers from the luncheon so the residents could enjoy them later, but she'd made no arrangements to pick them up. Mrs. Williams had assured her she could stop by anytime she wanted. But how she had ended up here now was beyond her.

"Call me if you need a ride to your next appointment," Heidi had told her mother when she'd pulled up to the curb.

"Don't worry, I'm sure I can find a bus," Alice had

answered quietly. "I wouldn't want to bother you any more than I already have."

The closing of the car door had seemed like a loud finale to an awkward afternoon, even though her mother hadn't slammed it.

Now Heidi stood in the waning afternoon light, staring at the modern nursing-home facility and wondering if her mother could have been right. Had she treated her family as if they were a bother? As if she were somehow better than they were?

She'd read somewhere lately that a greater proportion of women chose to marry men with whom they shared much in common rather than marry up, as they had once been more likely to do. And if a woman did marry up, it was necessary for her to leave behind the life she had known to avoid clashes.

She opened the nursing home's door and stepped inside, welcoming the cool air.

"Heidi!" Mrs. Williams greeted her, instantly coming from the nurses' station. "Good to see you again. I hadn't expected to see you so soon."

"Don't worry if the trays aren't ready. I was just in the neighborhood and thought I'd stop by."

"Oh, no, they're ready, all right. Everything was gone the same day. Come on, I'll show you where I stored them."

Heidi followed her, passing through the day room where a few of the residents she recognized from the party sat, a couple of them playing cards, others in quiet conversation. Mrs. Williams opened the kitchen door and then pulled Heidi's trays from under a table.

"There."

Heidi thanked her. "I hope everyone found the food satisfactory."

"Satisfactory? They all took your name and number for future events, so don't be surprised if you get at least another couple of bookings before the month's out."

Heidi smiled. "Thank you."

"No, thank *you*. The residents loved you."

"Speaking of lovers," Heidi asked after they'd walked back to the main corridor, "I was wondering if I could look in on the birthday boy."

Mrs. Williams paused, her face drawing into solemn lines. "Basile? Oh, I'm sorry, sweetie, but he's left us."

Heidi's footsteps slowed. "Where'd he go?"

The nurse gave her a soft smile. "The morning following his birthday we found him sleeping peacefully. A sleep from which he never awakened." She shook her head slightly. "I swear, even in death, he wore that wicked little grin."

Heidi felt stunned. Basile was dead? That was impossible.

No, not impossible. She just hadn't expected it to happen so soon after she'd met him.

"Do you have his funeral arrangements?" she asked Mrs. Williams.

"Sure, honey. Let me go get them for you."

Heidi stood alone in the hall, feeling as if the walls were growing farther and farther away, the length longer. She purposely moved to her right, near the wall, and leaned her elbow against it as if for support.

"Are you all right?" Mrs. Williams asked after she'd handed her a slip of paper.

Heidi nodded, although she felt anything but okay. "Fine. It's been a long day, that's all."

The nurse nodded in understanding. "It's always a bit of a shock when the more lively ones go. Like there's a hole in your life somehow."

Heidi held up the slip of paper. "Thanks."

"Don't mention it, sweetie. Maybe I'll see you there."

17

HEIDI SCRUBBED and scrubbed and scrubbed until the professor's house shone like a new copper penny. Not a book was left undusted, an inch of wood unpolished. She'd turned her cell phone off, turned the radio up, and set about the mindless physical activity until every muscle in her body ached and her brain was numb and completely free from thought.

As she knelt in the middle of the kitchen floor and peeled off her rubber gloves, she was accosted by the memory of her mother. Not from today. But from long ago. Of her mother doing much the same thing Heidi had just done, her hair tied up in a bandana, carrying a bucket filled with soapy water around the house until every last thing had been cleaned.

Could her mother have been doing the same thing Heidi was now? Trying to exorcise her problems with a few hearty scrubs with a brush?

Of course, Heidi knew that nothing would accomplish that. But it did help her to put distance between then and now and, she hoped, it would allow her to get a better handle on everything.

She lifted herself from the floor, emptied the bucket in the sink and stared at the clock. After eleven.

She felt it should have been three in the morning.

She stared at the counter tile grout (Q-tips would do the trick), but stopped herself short. She was done. The skin on her hands felt as if it might slough off under the water she ran over them, her knees had bright-red spots where she'd been on all fours. Her body refused more abuse.

She finally shut off the running faucet, gently wiped her hands on a towel and then picked up her cell from the kitchen table and switched it on. Three messages. Hoping one might be from her mother, she pressed the button for her voice-mail box and listened.

"What's up, babe? Hey, I'm going to be tied up tonight with some last-minute problems on the site. I'll see you tomorrow."

Heidi grimaced and pressed the button to delete the message.

"Heidi? Hi, this is Mrs. Williams from the retirement home."

She saved the message and listened for the third.

"Never mind. Goodnight."

Kyle.

She looked at the display to double check the number accompanying the message. Definitely Kyle. And he'd called a half hour ago.

What had he wanted to say? She felt an urge to find out.

Instead, she clapped the phone closed and put it back on the table, then headed for the shower, where she scrubbed herself with as much fervor as she had the house.

She'd always been so damn sure of herself. What she wanted. Where she was headed. And exactly how she was going to get there. Jesse. School. Catering. Hell, she'd been upset when Jesse had proposed to her six months before he was supposed to, and she had turned him down, sending him away with clear instructions on when she wanted him to do it. And indicating that it had better be in a unique, memorable way. Something she could share with their grandchildren.

So long as there was someone to blame for her lot in life, then there was some way she could change it. But if she had only herself to blame…

She winced as she gingerly dried herself off.

Leaning against the bathroom sink, she sighed. As exhausted as she was, her brain still refused to shut down. Over and over again she turned everything around in her mind, searching for a clue, an answer, anything to help her get a handle so she could pull herself safely through the mud her feet were mired in.

She tossed the towel to the floor in the corner and went to get dressed. There was no way she was going to go to bed now.

At least not in her own bed.

KYLE SAT at his drafting table in his downstairs den, the four-bedroom house far too quiet. The last CD he'd fed to the player must have finished some time ago without his realizing it.

He dropped his pencil in the tray and rubbed his forehead. There was no rush on the plans he was working on, but going up to bed was out of the question, no matter how early he had to get up in the morning.

He switched off the table lamp and meandered into the hall and then into the kitchen at the back of the house. He'd built the place to suit him and him alone, although he admitted to having had thoughts of kids running around it at some point in the future. Every detail bore his thumbprint.

He was aware that having been raised without a home had made it important to him to have one of his own. It had probably played a large role in his wanting to be an architect. But none of that took anything away from the fact that he loved this place. Although he'd been told it could use a woman's touch.

He switched on the light above the kitchen island and grabbed a bottle of beer and the other half of the roast-beef sandwich he'd made earlier but hadn't finished. He sat on a stool at the granite counter and switched on the small plasma television set suspended above the island so that it could be turned to be viewed from anywhere in the room. The local news was on. Not much happening. Which was good, he supposed. Although he could have used something to take his mind off things. Something to remind him that the world didn't revolve around him and his desire for his best friend's girl. No matter that that same best friend was probably in another woman's arms at that moment.

He washed down a bite of the roast beef with beer then sat for long moments staring at his solo reflection in the kitchen window over the sink. His face was drawn into long lines, his shoulders were curved inward under his black T-shirt. Five o'clock shadow had progressed so that it was visible even in the blurry glass.

Sometimes he caught his reflection and wondered who the guy was looking back at him. Especially lately. He was acting in a manner unfamiliar to him.

He pushed the sandwich away again. Much of the reason he'd come to Fantasy was to live the life he'd always fantasized about. Become a successful architect, a good husband, and, he hoped, a good father.

While he might have achieved his first goal, the other two were nowhere in his sights. Not while he was holding a torch for another man's woman.

Car headlights cut a swath across his backyard, and the quiet of the house allowed him the luxury of hearing someone pulling up his drive. It wasn't just another turn-around, which he was used to getting this far out of town, because the lights would have cut back the other way and the sound of the engine would have disappeared.

Grabbing his beer, he went to the front door and opened it. He was surprised to see Heidi's car pulling to a stop. He hit a button and the far garage door opened. She appeared to hesitate and then pulled in. He pushed the button to close it and walked to the door off the kitchen that led to the garage.

She climbed out of her Sunfire and looked around, watching as the garage door closed behind her.

"Thanks," she said.

Kyle took a long pull from his beer. He'd have preferred if she'd refused the offer of anonymity and had left her car in the drive. But she hadn't.

She came to stand in front of him wearing a pair of shorts and a T-shirt and flip-flops, as if she'd gotten dressed in a hurry. Her hair was damp, most likely from a shower since the night was clear and warm.

"Hey," she said quietly.

"Hey, yourself." He was reluctant to motion for her to come inside.

In that one moment he understood an incredible urge to ban her from invading the last untouched part of his life. She'd dropped Jesse off at his place, and picked him up there, but she'd never been inside. And he suddenly wanted to keep it that way.

"I got your message."

He rubbed his forehead with the back of the hand holding the beer. "I didn't leave one."

She smiled slightly. "I know."

She looked around again at the contents of his garage, at the pickup truck he used for work, and the late-model sedan he drove during his off hours. In the far corner, next to her car, stood an old Harley he took out every now and again. "You ride?"

"Sometimes."

"Would you take me for a ride?"

He took his time eyeing her from the tip of her tousled hair to her scarlet toenails. "You're not dressed for it."

"Oh."

She looked uncomfortable standing there staring up at him.

"Is there something you wanted, Heidi?" he asked.

She cleared her throat. "I thought you were the one who had something to say."

"In the light of day. At the café."

"Why not here?"

Why not here, indeed.

How did he tell her he didn't want her to invade this last little piece of himself? He wanted to continue walking through his house without remembering how she looked sitting in a particular chair, or how she smelled when she passed him, or what she said.

And she smelled good. The scent of her shampoo and soap teased his nose and wreaked havoc with his intention to bar her from his home.

His answer to her was a shrug and another slug of his beer.

"Oh, for God's sake," she said, edging her way by him. "Mona's not here because you would never have opened your garage door for me if she were."

"How do you know that?"

She squinted at him. "Is she?"

"No." He pushed away from the jamb and closed the door, resigned to the fact that he was damned to live out the remainder of his life with reminders of this woman stamped all over. Perhaps it was part of the price he was meant to pay for his transgressions.

Probably it meant he was a fool ten times over.

"So what did you want?" she asked, following him into the kitchen. "You know, when you called."

"I dialed the wrong number."

"Sure you did."

She took the stool he'd been sitting on and eyed his leftover sandwich.

"Am I interrupting dinner?"

He took another stool two up from her. "No. I'm done."

"Do you mind, then? I'm suddenly famished."

His gaze lingered on the smooth length of her bare legs. Suddenly, he was, too. But not for food.

"Mmm, this is good. Did you get the meat from Barber's?"

"I actually picked it up from a place in Toledo. Monnette's?"

"I know it. I get a lot of my produce from there. I didn't know their meat was good, though."

"Good enough, I suppose."

God, but the woman was going to be the death of him. She didn't have a clue what just sitting there watching her eat was doing to him. He'd changed into a pair of drawstring pants earlier and the fabric did little to hide the tent he was beginning to make with a certain part of his anatomy.

Heidi's chewing slowed and she wiped the side of her mouth with her pinky. She swallowed. "I want to apologize for the way I behaved earlier, you know, when you came to the café. It was an awkward time for me."

He shrugged.

She looked at the sandwich, her eyes clouding over. She put the food down and pushed it away much the way he had a few minutes earlier, as if remembering she was on a diet or that she didn't like horseradish. Although he suspected her reasons were more concrete than that.

She crossed her arms on the counter, looking at their reflection in the kitchen window. "God, you wouldn't believe the day I've had."

"Yes, I would."

She blinked at him.

"I've pretty much had the same thing for the past week."

She stared down at the counter, rubbing her thumb against the shiny surface.

"Do you mind if we don't talk?" she whispered.

"What did you have in mind?"

"I just want…" She swallowed hard and then cleared

her throat. "I just want to sit…" she looked at him, making a valiant effort to hide the moisture that shone in her brown eyes. "You know, if it's all right with you."

He considered her for a long moment, his heart beating loudly in his chest.

"No, it's not," he said.

She looked a blink away from bawling.

"I'd rather give you the hug you look like you need more than anything in the world."

And he drew her into his arms…

18

HEIDI MELTED into Kyle, stung by his initial denial to let her stay and relieved by his offer to hold her.

How long had it been since someone had just held her? Just wrapped his arms around her and hugged, expecting nothing in return? She couldn't remember.

Then again, she couldn't recall the last time she'd needed to be held.

And in that moment she so needed holding.

She took a deep breath, burrowing her nose deeper into the soft cotton of Kyle's T-shirt, absorbing his warmth. His hands slowly stroked her back up to her neck and down to the waist of her shorts. His breath caressed her ear as he nuzzled his chin in her hair, drawing her even closer.

God, what was she doing? She tightly closed her eyes, all the emotion that had been swirling within her building to a sort of crescendo that threatened to make her collapse. She shouldn't be here. She knew that. She also knew that it felt so damn good to be wanted by someone. Someone who didn't ask her questions, someone from whom she hid nothing, and someone who accepted her as she was. In every other aspect of her life it seemed as if something was expected of her.

Not here. Not now.

It was overwhelming to just feel…real.

"That bad, huh?" Kyle asked.

Heidi realized that some minutes had passed since he'd first taken her into his arms. But he wasn't asking her to move. Didn't appear to be uncomfortable. "Yes," she whispered.

"Do you want to tell me about it?"

Heidi shook her head. "No."

She felt his smile against her hair. "I might be able to help you work it out."

She pulled back slightly to gaze into his handsome face. "It might prove the proverbial straw that completely breaks me."

The somber shadow in his eyes told her he understood. "I see."

He drew her closer again and she gladly went, wishing with everything she was that she could just slide right under his skin. Become one with him so she was no longer alone. Wouldn't have to confront her problems, much less feel pressed to solve them.

She wasn't sure when it happened, but she felt something different in Kyle's touch. His hands dipped a little lower on her back until his fingertips teased the top of her panties inside her shorts. His mouth was no longer against her hair but on her neck. He wasn't kissing her, but his hot breath and slow movements told her he'd like to be.

She shifted, the heat on the outside of her seeping in, suffusing the dark storm within her with yellow light. Without lifting her head, she tunneled her hands under his T-shirt, reveling in the feel of his hard abs against her palms. He drew in a sharp breath, heightening her own sense of awareness.

He finally kissed her neck, sending shivers fluttering over her skin.

She scooted even closer, pressing her hips in between his legs so that she could feel his hardening member. She worked her hands around to his back, her breasts flattening against the wall of his chest through their clothes.

Then they were kissing…

Heidi wasn't certain who had initiated the act. It could have been Kyle, who threaded the fingers of his right hand through her hair and brought her face-to-face with him. It could have been her, as she stared into his eyes, wanting to drown in their depths.

He slid his lips against hers one way, then the other, nibbling at the corners of her mouth. Heidi closed her eyes, submitting completely to his will even as she clutched his back tightly.

Then his tongue entered her mouth and he kissed her lingeringly. Kissed her until she was breathless with need.

"Are you sure you want this?" he asked quietly, drawing slightly back and resting his forehead against hers.

"There's a lot I'm unsure of right now, but this," she kissed him. "This is one thing I can say I want unequivocally."

Kyle groaned and slid his hands up her back until he cupped the back of her head, holding her close, holding her still as he launched a hungry campaign against her mouth.

Heidi's knees threatened to give out from under her.

"God help me, but I didn't want to let you through

that door," he whispered harshly between kisses. "I can't take this any longer, Heidi. Can't take not knowing if I'll ever hold you again. Ever make love to you."

His words touched her as profoundly as his physical attention.

"No. Don't say anything. I couldn't bear it if you told me something I don't want to hear."

Heidi kissed him instead.

He got up from the stool and took her hand. "Come on. I want to make love to you in a bed. My bed. At least once."

She followed him, barely seeing the house around her as they climbed the stairs to the second floor and then walked down a long hall to the master bedroom. Kyle flicked a switch that lit two lamps sitting on either side of a king-sized bed. The light wasn't overly bright. Rather, the lamps cast a soft, yellow glow that was enough to allow her to see the striking planes of his face as he stood to face her at the side of the bed, but not so bright as to shake her from the cloud of passion that was thickening around her.

He lifted his hands to cup either side of her face and resumed kissing her, treating her as if she were breakable. Heidi took off her shorts and panties and then reached for the tie to his drawstring pants even as he freed her of her top and bra. Each movement seemed to flow easily into the next, as if the moment were predetermined. Kyle pulled back the top bedding and laid Heidi down on the mattress, cool softness buffeting her back even as his hot hardness covered her front. She ran her hands up over his rock-hard biceps, then inward to his pecs. He leaned to open the bedside drawer. It wasn't difficult to imagine what he was after. But he didn't immediately sheath himself. Instead, he held himself above her, taking her in.

Heidi smiled. She loved when he looked at her that way. As if he was afraid that if he looked away she might not be there when he looked back. She shifted her hand up to cup his jaw, thinking how unfair all this was to him. Where once she'd accused him of taking advantage of her, now she understood that it had been she who had taken advantage of him. While she had a lot to lose, he had just as much, if not more.

It was then, as he bent to claim her mouth, that she knew what she had to do. She had to break from both men. She needed to break things off with Jesse because...

Because she didn't love him anymore. Or, rather, she was no longer in love with him. She'd always love him. But her growing feelings for Kyle proved that she no longer viewed him in a way that could stretch on to forever.

While Kyle...

Her breath caught in her throat as she snaked her arms around him and held him tightly against her.

Kyle was a man she shouldn't allow herself to have. A man who had so very much to give a woman who wouldn't cause him problems. A woman who could give back without reservation, not just in moments of passion, but always. And where she stood now...well, she couldn't promise that to anyone. And she wasn't sure when she would be able to again, if ever.

She felt Kyle's hand on her inner thigh and she opened to him. Not just physically, but emotionally. When the backs of his fingers brushed her bare womanhood, she came up off the bed, the simple touch setting her ablaze with need. She kissed him deeply, moving her feet so that she could cradle him between her legs even as she reached for the condom she'd seen him place on the side table.

He lifted himself on his arms and gazed down at her as she put the foil packet between her teeth and opened it. Within moments, she was smoothing the lubricated latex down his stiff shaft, watching as his neck muscles strained against the flutter of her touch.

She positioned the thick tip against her slick opening, biting her bottom lip in anticipation.

When he entered her in one long stroke, she moaned in sweet surrender.

Where their meetings had been hot and rushed before, now…now the slow seductiveness of their love-making suffused her every cell, making her feel like one trembling, needy mass.

He withdrew and slid into her to the hilt again, edging her further up into the yellow-red tornado swirling within her.

Sweet mercy. She couldn't remember feeling so utterly connected to someone. So in tune. She couldn't be sure where she ended and where he began.

Kyle withdrew completely. She made a sound of protest that rested in her throat when he sat back on his feet, coaxing her up until she sat in his lap, her legs circling his hips. She slid her arms around his neck as he entered her again, the new position stroking her in all the right ways.

She smoothed his hair back and dropped her mouth to his shoulder, catching his slightly salty skin between her teeth before kissing him in the same spot. He thrust upward again and she threw her head back, liquid fire filling her veins.

She didn't know how it was possible for two separate people to fit together so perfectly. Finding her footing behind him, she slid up his long shaft and then sat back down again, tilting her hips inward to take him in fully. He licked her breast, catching her nipple in his mouth. He bit down gently and then sucked.

Heidi shivered all over, running her hands through the back of his hair.

Kyle grasped her hips, shifting her forward and then back and then lifting her. When he brought her back down, she met his thrust.

She gasped, feeling orgasmic yet not ready to surrender to the ripples rolling through her. She cracked her eyes open, watching him watch her, his eyes dark orbs in the dim light. He seemed resolved to draw this out for as long as possible. As if afraid this might be their last time.

Heidi clutched him tightly, her throat closing as she realized that this *would* be their last time. She had to release Kyle from whatever it was that they shared. Had to free herself from all romantic attachments so she might have time to figure out what had happened to her.

Had to learn to be by herself for a while.

If she didn't know better, she would have thought Kyle had picked up on her tumultuous thoughts. His hands on her hips strengthened, his thrusts were more powerful, as if he were determined to force all thought from her mind.

He succeeded.

Heidi followed his lead, increasing the rhythm of her movements until her flesh slapped against his, her breasts swaying wildly, the world fading to red as she took him again and again and again.

Oh, yes…

When the first waves hit her, she was rendered completely incapable of movement. She stretched her calves out behind him, her feet elevated even as her hands clutched him. He entered her, kissing her face then her mouth, demanding she experience the moment with him. She complied, only realizing after they collapsed to the mattress that she was silently crying.

19

KYLE LAY quietly, unable to believe he held a sleeping Heidi in his arms. He'd never dared even think the prospect within the realm of possibility. Yet there she was. Her soft snores the only sound in the dark room.

They'd spent the past hour making love, and after their last session she'd drifted off, her warm bottom curved against him. After a few minutes he'd turned onto his back and she'd instinctively rolled over to lay her head against his chest.

Lord, give me strength, he silently prayed.

He'd feared that the moment he let her inside his house, he'd be a goner. And he was afraid he was right.

He ran his fingertips over the warm silk of her back down to her pert bottom and then back up again. How many times while building this house had he imagined her there? Thought about what she might like and what colors she would choose?

Too many.

Of course, back then, she'd been merely representative of a vague, unreachable someone that he used to symbolize the woman he might one day marry.

And now that he had the woman herself…?

Kyle felt as if his heart might bruise his rib cage with

its furious beating. He knew a joy so great that she might consider sleeping with him in this bed forever.

He knew a fear so ominous that she might walk out the front door forever.

He closed his eyes and rubbed them with his free hand.

The situation was untenable. His options few. Heidi held all the cards. And knowing he'd given them all to her didn't help matters.

A swath of light cut across the bedroom ceiling. He squinted at it, waiting for it to disappear. Instead, it grew larger.

Another late-night visitor.

He gently shifted Heidi and got up, going to stand next to the front window.

Jesse.

He prayed for a different kind of help altogether.

"What's the matter?" Heidi's sleepy voice reached out to him as he got dressed.

"Nothing. Go back to sleep."

She sat up, the top sheet draping to her waist, the light from the moon washing her in gold.

A car door slammed and an instant later Jesse was knocking at the front door.

Heidi snatched the bedsheet up to cover herself. "Is it Mona?"

"Mona?" Kyle cursed under his breath. "No."

"Then who?"

"Just stay here."

Kyle didn't have time to explain things. In two minutes flat his friend would gain entrance to the house by hook or by crook, never one to be put off by a locked door. It went back to their college days when Jesse would find himself without a key.

Shrugging into his shirt, he hurried down the stairs in his bare feet and opened the door a scant second after Jesse's next bout of knocking.

"Oh!" Jesse stumbled backward, obviously inebriated, his hair disheveled, his equilibrium off. He grinned stupidly. The only thing missing was a big "hic" and stars hovering over his head. "There you are. Hope you don't mind, but I saw the lights on and decided to stop in for a, um, visit."

Not unlike Heidi hours before, Jesse edged his way inside without waiting to be invited.

Kyle ran his hand through his hair, staring at his friend with barely contained agitation. Jesse picked up a statue of a horse on the hall table and stared at it as if it were the first time he'd seen it though it had been there since Kyle moved in.

He thought of asking Jesse to leave. Hint that he had a woman upstairs. But he was half afraid that in Jesse's state, and given the amount of time since Kyle had been without a woman, his friend might rush the stairs to verify that such a person existed.

"Looks like you need some coffee," he said instead, leading the way toward the kitchen.

"No," Jesse said, putting the horse down. "What I need is a beer."

"I'd say you've had one too many of those."

Since it was after two, his friend had probably closed down whatever bar he'd been at.

Kyle put on coffee.

"She put me out, man." Jesse took a stool at the

island and stared at the half-eaten sandwich in front of him.

Kyle slanted a wary glance toward the doorway, wondering how far his friend's voice carried. Could Heidi hear him? If she could, what would she make of what he was saying?

Damn.

He hadn't had a chance yet to speak to his friend about the Mona situation. Partly because he wasn't looking forward to a conversation they'd had countless times back in Boston. Mostly because he wasn't in much of a position to preach to anyone, considering his and Heidi's extracurricular activities.

"You're right," Kyle said. "You need a beer."

He rounded the island and slapped his friend on the shoulder a little harder than was necessary to distract him from saying anything else on the Mona matter. There was no way he was giving him anything else to drink. If he had his way, he'd take him straight home where he could sleep it off.

"Hey! What was that for?" Jesse's voice slurred.

"Come on, buddy. I'm all out of beer, so let's go get some."

"Beer. Yeah. I need a beer…"

HEIDI PACED the upstairs hall in a panic. Jesse was there? Was he looking for her? Had he finally caught them?

She gripped the railing banister and leaned over, trying to hear what was going on in the kitchen even as she clutched the sheet to her breasts.

"She…out, man."

Jesse's voice, for sure. After he'd had one too many.

Did he mean her? But she hadn't talked to him that night. And it was now after 2:00 a.m.

"Come on, stop messing around," she heard Kyle say a few minutes later, his voice sounding closer. Too close for comfort.

She spotted him coming into the hall and jerked backward and out of the line of sight.

Holy cow! That was close.

"Hey, you don't mind my coming so late, do you?"

Heidi inched her way back down the hall so that she was in easy escape distance of the bedroom.

"Of course not. Why would I mind?"

"I mean, I saw the lights on and everything, so I figured…"

Heidi swallowed thickly.

"Come on, let's go get that beer," Kyle said.

Yes, go! Go get that beer.

"You got a girl up there, don't you?" Jesse said.

Heidi's eyes flew open in terror. She weighed her options. If she went back to the master bedroom and Jesse came up, she was sure to be caught.

She eyed the other rooms, choosing the one closest to her. It looked like a guest bedroom.

"Yes, well, according to you it should be Mona."

Jesse groaned. "Don't even mention Mona, man…"

Heidi craned her neck so she could hear. What about Mona?

The front door slammed and she heard a racket then inventive cursing from Jesse.

"This is the sidewalk," she heard Kyle say as if to a child. "This is a bush."

Moments later a car engine started. Heidi rushed to

the bedroom and stood off to the side of the window, watching as Jesse's truck backed down the drive with Kyle at the wheel. When they disappeared down the road, she knew a relief so complete, so absolute that she sank to the floor and leaned against the wall, still clutching the sheet to her chest.

The last person she would have expected to show up at Kyle's at that time of night was Jesse. She'd been terrified he'd gone by her place to find her not home and had headed to Kyle's to look for her.

Which, of course, was dumb, because Kyle's house wouldn't even have shown up on the top one hundred places where she might be.

Unless he was on to them...

Heidi struggled to a standing position, discarding the sheet when it impeded her progress, and quickly got dressed. She needed to get out of here, fast.

Once she was standing in the kitchen on her way to the garage, she hesitated. She should leave a message for Kyle.

She found a pad of Post-it notes on the refrigerator. She took one off and looked for a pen, finding one in the first drawer she pulled open.

"Kyle," she wrote.

Her hand hovered above the yellow paper.

What should she say?

"Hey, babe, thanks for the great, no, unforgettable night."

She cringed, recognizing that as something Jesse might say to her.

"Dear Kyle, Thanks for saving my bacon..."

But by saving hers, he was also doing himself the same service.

"Kyle, Goodbye…"

The word reverberated in her mind.

She knew that's what she should do. With little ceremony. No explanation beyond the obvious. She should finally end this chaos once and for all.

It wasn't fair to keep him dangling. No matter how much she longed for his companionship, his nearness, until she figured out who this new, emerging Heidi was, she couldn't promise anything beyond the moment. She looked around her, taking in every meticulous detail of his kitchen and the rest of the house beyond. Everything spoke of comfort and stability and of a future that included family.

It was clear that Kyle wanted much more than one-night stands.

It would have to come from someone else, not her.

The knowledge cleaved her heart in two. But what could she do other than break things off? A scant two weeks ago she'd believed herself in love with Jesse and was speeding full steam ahead toward a future with him. A future of marriage, children. Was it even possible for her to now want that same thing with Kyle? How could she trust that? How could he trust her?

He couldn't.

She left the note with just his name on it and quickly raced out of the house before she could change her mind.

20

The Party...

SATURDAY MORNING—Jesse's birthday—loomed bright
and warm, but might as well have been a rainy day in
February for all Heidi noticed. She drove to Jesse's
parents' house early, the back of her car filled with the
items she'd made that morning and the raw materials
for food that still needed to be fixed. She'd already
transported a criminal amount of food to the Gilbreds
over the past couple of days, storing it in their refrigerator and pantry with strict instructions that they were
to ban Jesse from the kitchen should he stop by, which
he was known to do. Mrs. Gilbred had suggested they
tell him they'd had the place fumigated and nothing was
fit to eat until she could clean and restock.

Heidi didn't know if Jesse's mother had had to utilize
the excuse. She'd barely said five words to Jesse since
picking him up from his trip to Boston.

Something niggled at the edge of her mind, a low
whisper that she batted away as effectively as a gnat
buzzing around her head. Which was to say not at all. It
kept circling back around, growing louder, then disap-
pearing for a little while, only to return with a vengeance.

It was something Jesse had said to Kyle last night. Or, rather, something Kyle had said to Jesse:

Yes, well, according to you it should be Mona.

She tried to remember Jesse's response, but couldn't.

She pulled into the Gilbreds' driveway and drove around back, where Jesse's sisters were already busy at work with the decorations. Heidi looked around, not realizing what—or rather, whom—she was looking for until she didn't see him.

Kyle wasn't there yet.

It was just as well. She had enough to do without reliving last night.

"Heidi!" Liz called, putting down a roll of blue crepe paper and coming to the car to help her take things out of the back. "I'm sorry I wasn't able to help more," the pretty blonde said. "Things have been insane at the firm lately."

"That's all right," Heidi said. "In a few hours this will be all over with, everyone will have enjoyed themselves, and we'll sit around stuffed to the gills smiling at a job well done."

Liz smiled and wagged her finger at her. "I like the way you think, girl."

With the two of them working together, Heidi had everything unloaded in no time and she took over the kitchen, with strict orders for no one to come inside. Of course, those orders were disobeyed at every turn. If little Jasmine wasn't sneaking a piece of cheese from a tray, Jesse's father Clyde was grabbing a radish carved to look like a rose.

"Everything looks lovely, dear," Jesse's mother Bonnie said a short time later as she, too, entered the kitchen. But she went for the coffeemaker in the corner rather than the trays.

"Thanks, Mrs. Gilbred."

Bonnie stepped a little closer, considering the array of food. "You are really very good at this, aren't you?"

With no client menu to adhere to, Heidi had gone a bit wild, fixing anything and everything that came to mind. "I enjoy what I do."

"It shows."

Clyde appeared in the doorway. "Where's my tennis racket?"

The sharp expression on Bonnie's face surprised Heidi. "How would I know?" The smile she gave Heidi looked tight and forced. "Men. They wouldn't know how to put their pants on if not for us."

"I can put my pants on just fine. It's my tennis racket and your penchant for hiding it on me that's at issue here."

"Perhaps if it were tennis that was taking up all your time lately, I'd be handing it to you right now and wishing you a nice match."

For the first time in her years-long relationship with the older couple, Heidi felt uncomfortable. "I'll, um, just go take a couple of these trays outside…"

Bonnie took a sip of her coffee. "Don't be ridiculous, Heidi. If you're going to be a part of this family, then you should know the sordid truth."

Clyde grumbled under his breath and left the room. Moments later, the front door slammed and both Bonnie and Heidi jumped.

Bonnie casually walked to a cabinet, took down a bottle of Irish cream, and added a healthy dollop to her coffee. Heidi raised her brows, staring at the suddenly unfamiliar woman who took a long sip and then left the room, telling her to call if she needed any help.

Scant minutes earlier, she would have thought herself in the greatest need of help. Now she wasn't so sure.

She rested her hands against the counter and took several deep breaths, that voice playing around the edges of her consciousness again.

Could it be possible that the Gilbreds' thirty-year marriage was on shaky ground? She'd held them up for so long as the perfect example of the way she wanted her own life to play out that she couldn't wrap her mind around the possibility Jesse's parents were having problems.

She picked up a peeler and went to work on a carrot, squeaking when she took a bit of skin off her finger in the process.

She put the carrot and peeler down and took a deep breath. She didn't have the luxury of thinking about her own relationships just then, much less the Gilbreds'. She had a party to put on…

THIS WAS a disaster waiting to happen.

Kyle hung back from the boisterous party crowd, thinking that to the untrained eye, the goings-on in the Gilbreds' backyard looked like a regular American cookout celebration. There were dozens of guests in their summer duds milling about the lush surroundings, holding drinks and eating the sublime food Heidi had made. There was laughter and quiet conversation and soft music that he knew was going to kick up a notch a little later with a live band.

He scanned the crowd, his gaze settling on the guest of honor. Jesse looked nothing like the drunken sot that had landed on his doorstep last night, ruining Kyle's time with Heidi. To the contrary, he appeared the surprised, happy birthday boy with a great gal who spoiled him and not a care in the world.

Kyle wondered if the guy ever got hungover. If he did, he somehow managed to mask it behind his big, friendly grin.

"Hey, loverboy," a woman said next to him.

For a moment he was afraid Mona had found out about the party and had popped up unexpectedly to latch on to him as her fake date. Instead he found Jesse's sister Liz linking arms with him.

He smiled warmly at her, instantly relaxing. The fact that the family had once tried to match him with the gorgeous blonde didn't detract from the genuine affection they had for each other. All of Jesse's family felt like Kyle's family. And he and Liz shared a nice, brother/sister bond.

"Nice turnout," she commented, surveying the guests.

"Did you expect differently?"

Liz laughed. "As popular as Jesse is? No."

"Where's your date?" he asked.

"Jerry? He's around here somewhere." She glanced around the backyard. "Hey, I've finished renovating that apartment over my garage. If you hear of anyone needing a place, send them my way."

"I will." He pictured Liz living by herself in that large Tudor-style home in the older section of Fantasy. The idea of someone he or the family trusted renting the garage apartment made him feel somewhat better. She might be a successful trial attorney, but he worried about her.

Kyle tensed as he spotted Jesse standing with Heidi,

who appeared preoccupied keeping the tables well-supplied. He remembered the note she'd left him that morning. Rather, the partial note, because all she'd written was his name. Nothing else.

He was afraid that words hadn't been needed. That the previous night had been the last he'd spend with her. And there was nothing else to say.

"Oh, no. Don't look now, but here come my parents," Liz whispered.

Kyle glanced at her curiously, but there wasn't time to ask why this should be an event, because Bonnie and Clyde Gilbred were in front of them before he could blink.

"Kyle," Bonnie said, kissing him on both cheeks. "Glad to see you could make it."

He didn't know where else he might be. "Mrs. Gilbred."

"Not for long, if my divorce attorney has anything to say about it."

Kyle stared at her.

"Big guy," Clyde said, shaking hands with him and awkwardly doing the shoulder-bucking thing that he and Jesse did.

"Mr. Gilbred," Kyle acknowledged.

Next to him, Liz muttered, "Don't believe a word of the divorce thing. I just caught them going at it like rabbits on top of the washing machine not an hour ago."

She walked away, leaving Kyle to make of her words what he would.

HEIDI LOOKED at her watch for the tenth time, wishing the numbers would hurry up. It had been a long day already and it wasn't nearly half done. And if Jesse hugged her and thanked her again for the benefit of everyone around, she was going to scream.

Okay, so maybe that wasn't the most generous attitude to have on his birthday, but just as soon as this party was over, she was going to tell him their relationship was, too.

So she was probably being a little irrational. But the more Jesse hung around her, the more Kyle hung back. And the fact that she wanted Kyle closer made her all the more irritated.

Did that even make sense?

She swatted a bug away from her ear and stirred the potato salad where it sat on a bowl of ice.

Then there was that whole whispering-voice thing.

Just what in the hell had Kyle meant when he'd said that according to Jesse he should have been with Mona?

And speaking of Mona, why wasn't she here clinging to Kyle's arm?

She looked over at him again and found that Liz had claimed the spot instead, laughing good-naturedly with him about something. Then moments later, after Jesse's parents joined them, Liz left.

Heidi couldn't blame her. On the weird-happenings scale, the Gilbreds' odd behavior ranked right up there.

She picked up an empty serving plate and headed toward the door to the kitchen, nearly bumping into someone.

"Oh, excuse me," she said, stepping back.

She found herself staring straight at Mona.

Speak of the devil.

The other woman smiled back at her, looking radiant in a sexy red halter dress and strappy sandals. Heidi glanced down at her own white slacks and tank top.

It was decided: she hated Mona.

"We keep seeming to do that, don't we?" Mona said, smiling broadly. "Bumping into each other I mean."

That little voice in the back of Heidi's mind got a little louder. "Yes, I guess we do." She began to angle around the other woman. "Kyle's back over there somewhere. If you'll excuse me, I have something to get from inside."

"Kyle?"

Heidi slowed her step, wondering why Mona had said his name as if he were the last person she was interested in seeing.

"Oh, of course! Sorry. It's been a long day." Mona headed in the direction Heidi indicated.

Tell her about it.

"I NEED to speak to you."

Heidi gasped, jumping when Kyle appeared at her elbow fifteen minutes later as she was setting up the three-layer, chocolate-on-chocolate birthday cake on an outdoor table. She nearly dumped the cake onto the grass.

"This is so not the time or the place," she whispered.

"You're wrong. This *is* the time. And the place."

He grasped her elbow and began leading her away from the table.

Heidi was faced with one of two choices: allow him to guide her and smile at anyone watching them as if this was a normal event, or fight him and cause a suspicious scene.

She chose the former. While she intended to talk to Jesse, she'd prefer to do so after he blew out his candles.

She'd worked too hard on this event to let it fall apart around her ears.

Heidi smiled tightly at a couple she remembered from high school. "You are so in trouble for this."

Kyle leaned closer. "I accept the consequences."

He paused, as if uncertain where to take her.

"Not the house," she said. "People are in and out every couple of seconds."

She spotted the portable cabanas set up on the other side of the pool at the same time he did.

"Don't even think about it," she said, even as he began leading her in that direction.

She could imagine what people would say if they saw them entering the private enclosure together.

"You're right," he said, stopping. He looked at her, then his watch. "You go in first. I'll follow in a couple of minutes."

"Nothing doing."

"Then we're going to have this out here in front of God and the guests and your future in-laws."

"I no longer have future in-laws."

He hiked a brow.

"Well, I won't after tonight."

He gave her the male equivalent of an eye roll. "Go to the tent. Now."

Tent. It was a cabana.

He leaned closer to her as if he might kiss her.

Heidi went.

21

HEIDI WAITED in the white, four-by-four canvas change-room, feeling closed in and anxious. What did Kyle think he was doing? While they hadn't spoken since last night, she'd been relatively sure that he understood what would happen. The fact that he hadn't tried to contact her since told her that.

Then why was he arranging clandestine meetings in the worst of all public places?

The flap opened and Kyle stepped in, nearly scaring her out of her skin.

"Expecting someone else?" he said.

"Shhh." She placed a finger against his lips, and then snatched her hand back when the simple contact ignited a desire to touch more. "Someone might hear you." She looked around the cramped environs. "We may be shielded from view, but we can still be heard."

"Point taken," he said, his voice considerably lower.

The tent didn't leave much room for maneuvering. Heidi tried the best she could to keep from looking directly at him. With scant inches between them, she didn't trust herself not to kiss him.

"So out with whatever it is you need to say. It's time to sing to the birthday boy."

"I'd rather sock the birthday boy."

Heidi had to look at him then.

"You heard me." Kyle sighed and ran his hand through his hair. "Look, Heidi, I know that I handled all this completely wrong."

"Handled? You make it sound like what happened between us was some sort of scripted event."

"Perhaps it was."

She stared at him.

"I've known I wanted you for a long time now."

"Look, Kyle, I—"

"No. Please. Let me finish."

Heidi bit her bottom lip, anxious to be out of the cabana.

"You…me. You've existed in my mind since before we even met."

What was he saying?

He reached out and tucked a strand of hair behind her ear, resting his fingertips against her neck. "I think it was that second phone conversation we had. You know, when Jesse and I used to be roommates and you'd call for him…"

"And he wouldn't be there and I'd talk to you."

"Yes," he smiled at her affectionately. "This conversation was about your wanting to change your major from finance to business."

Heidi smiled in remembrance.

"You already had two semesters of finance but your heart just wasn't in it, no matter how hard you tried. And while it would have been quicker to get a finance degree, you'd always dreamed of owning your own catering company."

Oh, God, how she'd gone on. That night, they must have spoken for two hours.

If she had ever wondered why Kyle had taken the time out to talk to her when she couldn't seem to get her own boyfriend on the phone, she couldn't remember. But she did recall that particular conversation as being one of the most defining in her college years.

"You spoke with such passion. Tried to convince yourself otherwise because it wasn't the practical choice. You threw around statistics about how half of new businesses went under in the first year and how it was very important to you to be financially independent as quickly as possible…" He searched her eyes. "Do you remember?"

She nodded, looking down to find her hand had somehow come to rest against his chest. "Yes," she whispered. "I remember. I also remember how patient you were. You let me ramble on…"

"And then what did I tell you? Before we hung up?"

He'd told her to follow her heart.

And here she was, years later, doing exactly that.

At least in matters of business.

As for her personal relationships…

She couldn't think about that now. Wouldn't.

"Why are you bringing that up now?" she asked.

"Because I think it's important that you remember it, Heidi. I think it's important that you put everything that's gone before with everything that's happening now…and then consider it all from the perspective that I think I'm falling in love with you."

THERE, he'd said it.

For Kyle, the proclamation had been one of the most

difficult to make in his life. Some people were raised to easily throw the word *love* around. He'd watched Jesse and their other college buddies end conversations with their parents and girlfriends with either, "I love you," or the responsive, "I love you, too."

Meanwhile, Kyle had never uttered the words to anyone.

Until now.

"No, that's wrong," he said, gazing into her confused face. "I don't think I am, I know I am. And it's not something I can stop, or ignore. Not anymore."

"Kyle…"

He winced, watching as Heidi tried to wrap her practical mind around the emotional declaration. He'd known she would try to run from it. Just as she had from every other conversation he'd tried to have with her in the past few days. But he couldn't allow it now.

"I know you're going to need some time to work everything out, Heidi. I just wanted…no, needed for you to hear what I had to say. And once you've taken that time, straightened out things for yourself, I want you to know that my door is open."

Feminine laughter sounded outside the cabana behind him. Familiar feminine laughter. He looked over his shoulder and grimaced.

He leaned his head so that his cheek brushed against hers, his mouth next to the delicate shell of her ear. "But it's you who's going to have to come to me, Heidi. With no reservations. With no thoughts of temporary. I want you in my life."

He heard her swallow and lifted his opposite hand to her shoulder, caressing the smooth skin of her arm.

The tent wall to his left fluttered as someone entered the neighboring cabana. Again, the laughter.

Kyle felt everything soft inside him tense up.

Until Heidi slowly moved and came nose to nose with him.

For long moments he could do nothing more than return her seeking gaze.

Then she was kissing him.

Softly. Tentatively. In a tenderly explorative way that made his heart thrum.

"God, I can't keep my hands off you…" a male voice said.

Kyle opened his eyes. He hadn't been the one who'd said the words, although he easily could have been, two minutes into the future.

He watched Heidi's eyes narrow as she pulled away and looked at the cabana wall to her right.

A female shriek and then, "Jesse! Stop. I told you, I can't do this anymore. You've been stringing me on for years. It's time for you to make a commitment."

"Oh, Mona, please don't do this to me—"

Kyle closed his eyes and groaned. He'd known that Heidi would find out at some point. He just hadn't anticipated it would be so soon.

Heidi pushed her way past him and ripped open the door to the neighboring cabana.

"Heidi!"

Kyle stood back with his arms crossed, unable to do anything but watch. This was one situation he couldn't help his friend with. Not that he wanted to. Despite the pain on Heidi's face as she clued into the years'-long deception, he was glad everything was out in the open now.

Well, almost everything.

"Hi, babe." Even now Jesse thought he could somehow talk his way out of it. Kyle shook his head. "Kyle! Hey, buddy. Look who was looking for you. Mona here came into the wrong cabana and thought I was you."

"Because it's just so dark in there," Heidi said, pointing out the fact that the cabanas were white and the setting sun shone directly on them.

"You don't think...you can't possibly believe that Mona and I..."

Kyle looked at the other injured woman and found her a blink away from hauling off and hitting Jesse one.

Kyle said, "You might as well own up to everything, Jesse. We both heard you and Mona and there's no way you're going to get out of this."

Heidi stared at him. "You knew?"

He rubbed his jaw, feeling as if he'd been physically hit. "Where do you think Jesse was when you used to call all those years ago, Heidi?"

She looked around at everyone, slack-jawed.

Party guests had fallen silent and were discreetly drawing closer to get a better look.

Not that Heidi, Mona or Jesse seemed to notice, Kyle noted.

"Wait a minute. You both heard us?" Jesse looked at the two of them. "Where were you?"

"In the neighboring cabana," Heidi said. "Continuing something that's been going on for some time."

Kyle knew she'd said the words in anger, but the

moment they were out, a calmness seemed to descend on Heidi. A peacefulness he hadn't seen for a good long time.

He smiled to himself.

"You were boinking my fiancée?" Jesse demanded of Kyle.

"She's not your fiancée." Kyle held up his hands and began backing away. "And *boinking* doesn't fit. I love her."

Jesse launched himself at Kyle. Kyle tried to sidestep him, but Jesse knew all of his moves and anticipated his intention, hitting him straight on. Kyle felt his feet go out from under him and was only semi relieved when he felt the water of the pool beneath him rather than cement.

Jesse tried slugging him while they were in the water but Kyle held him off.

"You son of a bitch!"

Kyle lifted his foot and pushed Jesse away, then waded toward the edge of the pool to hoist himself out.

It was only when he was dripping a puddle onto the patio that he spotted Heidi. She was carrying the triple-decker chocolate birthday cake toward the pool. Jesse began to lift himself out…and Heidi dumped the cake onto his head, forcing him back in.

The guests erupted in laughter and applause.

"We are so over," Heidi said.

Then she turned and stalked away without giving Kyle another glance.

22

HEIDI NEEDED a place where no one could find her. Not Jesse. Not Kyle. Not any of her friends. She called in to ask Nina for a few days off, then she showed up at her mother's doorstep.

Alice didn't so much as blink when she opened the door and let her in, no questions asked.

That had been two days ago.

Heidi lay across her old bed, her teeth feeling as if they needed to be shaved, not brushed, her body odor offensive even to her. Not that it mattered. She'd barely left the room except for bathroom breaks and to get one or two things from the refrigerator.

But she knew the timer on her bout of self-pity was drawing to a close. Not even her mother was that patient.

She heard little Tyler run past the closed door then back again. Her sister Melody called for him to keep it down, that Auntie Heidi needed her rest.

Heidi groaned and threw her arm across her eyes, immediately assailed by her own stench as she did so.

She groaned and again held her arms stiffly to her sides.

Jesse had been seeing Mona the entire time he'd been in Boston.

The words echoed again and again in her mind. Over the past forty-eight hours, she'd combed through every memory, every trip, every conversation, scavenging for evidence of Jesse's double life. And in the process, all that they'd had together was tainted. Colored with a black brush that left her feeling desolate.

She'd nearly driven herself insane during her short time with Kyle. How had Jesse done it for years?

She forced herself to reach for her purse on the floor next to the bed. She fished around for her cell phone. The battery had been low when she'd shut it off on the drive from the Gilbreds' to her mother's and she hadn't turned it on again. Now she powered it up to find she'd missed twenty-eight calls. Most of them from Kyle. Many from Nina. A few from Jesse. And one from Liz.

She pressed the button to check for voice-mail messages and the cell went dead.

She flopped back down on the bed. Great. She finally decided to rejoin the land of the living, and the land of the living didn't want her.

Jesse had been seeing Mona the entire time he'd been in Boston.

The words circled back again, a mantra of sorts.

That was the real reason she hadn't been able to get through to him at his hotel that night. He'd probably stayed with Mona. Hell, Mona was probably the reason he'd traveled there.

Business.

She snorted.

So that meant Jesse was the reason Mona had come to Fantasy. Not Kyle.

She moaned. Then there were her own less-than-honorable antics with Kyle.

Had she really told Jesse balls-out that she'd been messing around with his best friend?

The bedroom doorknob jiggled. Heidi stiffened and listened for her mother's voice. Every couple of hours or so, Alice stopped and asked if she needed anything. And every couple of hours or so, Heidi told her no.

But this time the door opened a crack and a three-year-old face appeared.

"Auntie Heidi? Are you sleeping?"

For a moment, Heidi considered pretending that she was. But she was tired of pretending. Especially since it appeared she'd been doing it for years. She'd purposely looked away from the truth and headed toward a destination that was never hers to achieve.

She lifted herself up on her elbows and considered her nephew with a pang of sorrow. She'd already missed so much of his young life. Too much.

"Come in, Tyler."

He looked behind him and then came through the opening sideways, carefully closing the door after him.

Heidi patted the bed next to her. She hadn't realized how dark it was with the blinds closed on the window behind her bed. She reached back and tugged on the bottom of the blind, guiding it up a foot. Instantly, warm summer light infused the room. A room she might have considered dingy and unlivable such a short time ago. But now it was only a room.

"Come here."

Tyler did, shuffling his feet uncertainly then jumping to sit on the bed.

Heidi smiled, smoothing back his curly light-brown hair.

"Hi," he said.

"Hi, yourself."

"Are you dying?"

Heidi laughed softly. She might not be dying on the outside, but something very important to her had died on the inside.

"No," she told him. "I'm just sick, that's all. Have you ever been sick?"

He nodded, his eyes appearing huge in his small face.

"Do you remember being in bed for a long time, waiting to get better?"

He nodded again.

"Well, that's what Auntie Heidi's doing. She's getting better."

"Will you be better soon?"

Would she?

Heidi didn't know.

What she did know was that she'd spent so much time trying to climb her way to what she'd considered a better life that she'd missed too much in her real one.

A problem she intended to remedy.

"Do you know what my favorite color is?" she asked him.

He shook his head.

"It's purple."

He made a face. "Purple? That's a girl's color."

"In case you hadn't noticed, I am a girl." She ruffled his hair. "I bet I know what your favorite color is. I bet it's blue."

"It's green."

She felt a pang.

"Ty?" her sister's Melody's voice came from the hallway.

They both turned toward the sound, but neither of them moved, listening to Melody walk up the short hall then back again. Finally, there was a soft knock on the door.

Heidi leaned closer to Tyler. "Tell her to come in."

"Come in, Mommy!" he shouted.

Melody opened the door, looking upset.

"It's okay," Heidi said. "We were just visiting."

Melody held her hand out. "Come on, Ty. It's time for lunch."

Heidi caught his arm before he could climb from the bed. "Can I have a hug first?"

He threw his chubby little arms around her neck and squeezed. Heidi closed her eyes and hugged back.

"I love you, kiddo," she whispered into his soft hair.

"I love you," he said back.

She smiled into his face.

"You stink," he said.

Heidi burst out laughing as he ran, giggling, to his mother.

"ARE YOU leaving?"

Heidi had taken a shower and brushed her teeth and was standing in the kitchen making herself a peanut butter and jelly sandwich when her mother spoke behind her.

She allowed the knife to sink into the jelly. "I wasn't planning on it." She looked over her shoulder to find Alice with her arms crossed. Was it her imagination, or was her mother's baby bump beginning to show? "Unless you'd like me to."

Alice's shoulders relaxed and she uncrossed her arms. "No, no. Of course not. You're welcome here. Always. You may have forgotten that, but I never have."

Heidi winced and turned back to her sandwich. "Can I make you one?"

Melody had fed Tyler and was in her room putting him down for a nap. Heidi finished making her sandwich, skillfully cutting off the crust and slicing it in half before cleaning the counter of her mess and Melody's too. Strangely, she didn't mind.

"No. I'm fine. I can't seem to keep anything much down outside crackers nowadays."

Alice sat at the table and Heidi joined her after filling a glass with milk.

She'd finished half the sandwich in silence before Alice finally asked, "Are you going to tell me what happened?"

Heidi slowed her chewing, considering the question. She hadn't really confided in her mother during her initial courtship with Jesse in high school, or throughout their ongoing relationship. Now seemed a funny time to unload.

And, curiously enough, she didn't feel as if she needed to.

In some odd way, she was beginning to believe that things had worked out as they should have. As they were destined to.

She shook her head. "Not unless you really want to hear all the sordid details."

Alice looked at her for a long moment and then smiled. "I could do without those."

Heidi smiled back then continued eating.

"Just one question, Heidi." Alice looked at her intently, leaning forward to put her hands on the table between them.

Heidi finished her lunch and Alice reached for her hands, holding them tightly.

"Are you all right?"

Heidi's eyes welled with tears. "No. I'm not." She gave a watery smile. "But I will be."

Alice nodded. "Yes. I think you will."

A LITTLE LATER in the day, Heidi drove her old Sunfire to the Gilbred house. She'd left a mess the other night in more ways than one. And the easiest to clean up was the physical one.

The emotional one…

Well, her cell phone was charging in her car, buying her a little time in that department.

Or so she thought…

As she pulled the car into the Gilbreds' driveway, she immediately recognized Jesse's truck. Her heart skipped a beat in her chest.

Okay, so she hadn't banked on this. But she also wasn't the type to run away from a fight.

She sat for long moments, concentrating on her breathing. She didn't have a clue what she might say to him. She'd trust that the words would come when she needed them.

She got out of the car and went to the front of the house rather than the back, where she knew the family spent most of their time either in the yard or the air-conditioned sunroom.

Bonnie answered the door.

"Heidi!"

She looked much better than she had the other day. Heidi figured that the process of going through a divorce must agree with her.

"Hi, Mrs. Gilbred. May I come in?"

Bonnie looked behind her, then sighed and opened the door. "You might as well. Everything's out in the open now anyway, isn't it?"

Heidi wasn't sure she knew what Bonnie was talking about…until she walked down the long hallway and spotted Jesse in the sunroom sitting close to Mona, holding her hand. The two were talking about something and smiling.

The image was at once completely foreign, yet also natural.

And, surprisingly, Heidi didn't feel much of anything at all.

Shouldn't that worry her? Shouldn't she feel betrayed? Or at least hurt that the person she had thought was the love of her life was now in love with someone else?

Bonnie hesitated in closing the door.

"It's okay, Mrs. Gilbred. I'm not going to cause a scene." She shifted on her feet, considering the best course of action.

"The girls cleaned up everything. Lizzie took all the trays and tablecloths to her house. Said she'd get them back to you."

Heidi smiled. "Thanks." She cleared her throat. "Could you please tell Jesse that I'm here to see him?"

HEIDI couldn't help noticing how uncomfortable Jesse looked in the car next to her. He'd seemed reluctant to leave the house, but she'd reassured him that she needed to talk. And after all their time together, didn't they owe each other at least that?

"We should have taken my truck," he said now, trying to adjust the air-conditioning vent.

"That won't work. I need that freon you told me about."

He was sweating. But she wasn't entirely sure whether it was due to the hot summer temperature or his own sense of guilt.

Finally, she arrived at their destination. She pulled into the parking lot near the Huron River, shut off the engine and then got out of the car. The air felt cooler near the water and the thick canopy of trees that climbed the banks.

Jesse didn't follow.

Heidi poked her head inside her open window. "Don't worry. I don't plan to whack you on the back of the head with a tree branch and let your body float downriver."

He looked marginally relieved.

"Come, Jesse. This shouldn't take too long."

Of course, she'd severely underestimated his own need to cleanse himself of his sins.

As they sat on the river's edge, watching the occasional kayak and canoe float by, he told her how he'd met Mona. That he'd never thought it was anything but sex with her. And that he never meant to hurt anyone, especially not Heidi.

And Heidi told him about Kyle. Not much. But enough for him to understand that they'd been sleeping together for a short time. Long enough to have made an impact.

Heidi found she couldn't share details. Not like he

had with Mona. Everything was still too raw for that. And while Jesse appeared to have quickly accepted the end of their eight-year relationship and jumped feet-first into a new one with Mona, things weren't that simple for Heidi.

They reminisced about how they'd first met on the football field during practice their freshman year in high school, and how Heidi had made him meet her everywhere but her home. He hadn't known where she lived until a good year into their dating. And even though she'd shared many a dinner at his family's house, he'd never had one at hers. In fact, he'd only seen her mother and sisters on a handful of occasions.

Heidi mulled that over, feeling a shame that she'd never experienced before. Not shame for her family. Shame for herself.

"I don't know," she said quietly now. "I always thought I wasn't good enough for you. That I needed to try to be something better or else you might take a closer look and see me for who I really was and reject me."

Jesse scanned her face and then reached over to take her hand in his. It was one of the most sensitive and demonstrative gestures he'd ever made. Heidi blinked back tears.

"You were, are and always will be my first love, Heidi. It didn't matter if you came from the wrong side of town or Mars. Nothing would have changed how I felt about you."

She leaned her shoulder against his and squeezed his hand. "I guess that's something I never understood. Until now."

Had she somehow managed to smother what they'd had over the years by trying to mold herself into something different, something better than she'd judged herself to be? Had she been so busy being the perfect person, she hadn't relaxed and allowed herself to truly evolve into the person she was meant to be?

She laughed quietly, her throat tight with emotion. "I keep thinking I should be more upset about this. That I should be angry that you fooled around. That we're no longer going to be a couple…but I'm not."

Jesse leaned his head on top of hers. "I know. I feel the same. Strange, isn't it?"

She nodded, and the two of them stood contemplating the water for a long time without talking.

"You know, I'm glad you were my first love, Jesse. After all is said and done, I suppose in some roundabout way you've helped me become who I am and who I was meant to be." She smiled up at him. "Thank you for that."

"No, thank *you*, Heidi," he said quietly, his handsome face drawn into serious lines. He leaned in and kissed her. Softly. Lingeringly. One last time. "When you said you always thought you weren't good enough for me? Well, you're wrong, Heidi. It's you I was never good enough for…"

23

A month later...

KYLE STABBED the earth with the shovel and heaped the dirt next to the hole, the late-afternoon sun beating down on his back as he repeated the action, glad for the physical effort. It seemed to be the only thing capable of taking his mind off Heidi and the fact that a month had passed since he'd last seen her. Yesterday he'd finished putting up a wood slat fence on either side of his land. Today he was planting arborvitae trees along his back property line, both for privacy and to act as a windbreak.

Whoever said time healed all wounds should be taken out back and shot. If he was any example, time merely amplified the pain, leaving him an emotional wreck incapable of concentrating on anything that needed attention to detail. Which was just about every area of his life.

He stabbed the earth again. Where was she?

Common sense dictated that he try to accept that he might never see Heidi again. At least not in the way he wanted to.

Over the past weeks, he'd comforted himself with the knowledge that she and Jesse had, in fact, parted ways.

And if you listened to his friend, that parting had ultimately been amicable, despite the cake-on-the-head incident at the party. More than that, Jesse had evidently moved on, Mona by his side at every turn. In fact, Kyle saw more of Mona with Jesse than he'd ever seen of Heidi.

Of course, he recognized that his observation could have more to do with his dislike of Mona. She was overtly flirtatious, dressed provocatively and was Heidi's opposite in so many ways that he questioned if Jesse knew what he was doing.

Sex. That was it, pure and simple. He couldn't imagine his friend making any sort of solid future with the almost vulgar woman who had recently begun making noises about returning to Boston. Fantasy, Michigan, was obviously too small for her.

Not even the Gilbreds liked her, and the Gilbreds liked everyone. Kyle considered himself Exhibit One as proof of that.

So what did that mean, exactly? Could it be that the clandestine nature of Jesse and Mona's longtime affair had, in essence, fed on itself? That so long as things were hush-hush, the fires burned? And now that their relationship was more traditional, out in the open, did it stand a chance of making it beyond the six-month mark?

Kyle packed dirt around the root ball with his booted foot and grabbed the shovel.

If that were the case, then what did it say about any chance he might have with Heidi?

He paused, resting his gloved hand on the shovel handle as he wiped the sweat from his brow with his forearm. Maybe he should have waited until the weekend to do this. Morning would be the ideal time, before the late-summer sun had time set the air on fire. It probably wasn't a good idea to be out in this heat physically exerting himself.

The problem was he needed to do this now. If he didn't, he'd go insane inside the house by himself. Because, as he'd feared, everywhere he turned he saw Heidi. Heard her laughter in the halls. Fixed meals in the hope that that day would be the one when she'd finally show up. Rolled over in bed and reached for her, only to encounter cold sheets.

He started on the next hole with a violent shovel stab.

He'd gone by her place once. Her car hadn't been there, but he'd walked up to the back door anyway, figuring that if she were anywhere in the house, it would be in the kitchen.

Instead he'd seen an older man in a robe puttering around, pouring himself a cup of coffee while he read a newspaper.

Kyle had known panic at first. Then he remembered that the professor Heidi had been house-sitting for was probably due back. And that meant she'd moved on.

But where?

He'd thought twice about asking Jesse. While Jesse and Heidi might have parted on good terms, he and his friend…well, he didn't think it a good idea to push his luck.

Not that it mattered. He intended to do exactly as he'd promised. He wasn't going to go running after her anymore. It was up to her to come to him.

And if she didn't?

It was beginning to look more and more as if that was going to be the case.

"Hi."

Kyle stabbed the earth again and kicked his boot against the shovel's lip to force it farther into the soil. Great. Now he was hallucinating the sound of her voice out here. Before long, there would be nowhere to escape his obsessive need of her. Then where would he be?

"Kyle?"

He froze. The dirt on the shovel slid back down into the hole. Slowly, he turned.

He wasn't imagining things. Heidi was there. Looking like the devil in angel's clothing in a pair of white linen pants and a clingy purple shirt.

Every muscle in his body seemed to relax and tighten at once…

CALL HER stupid, but in all her introspection over the past four weeks, Heidi had completely left out Kyle's hotness factor. And how irrationally attracted to him she was.

The slanting sun was in his face and he had to squint to see her. He looked more than a little surprised. But he recovered quickly as he anchored the shovel in the soil next to him and leaned his forearm on it, considering her.

"Can we talk?" she asked when he didn't say anything.

He rubbed his chin with the back of a gloved hand. "Go ahead."

Heidi looked over her shoulder toward the house and air conditioning. Anywhere but at his tanned, well-defined abs. "Can we go inside?"

He appeared ready to refuse, to say he still had work to do. She braced herself.

She didn't know what she'd expected when she finally came to Kyle. Open arms, maybe? A big, warm grin? A passionate kiss that would lead to much more?

Instead, he was looking at her as if she might be the dirt on the bottom of his boot and was considering the wisdom of brushing her off.

He tugged one of his gloves off, then the other, and tossed them next to the shovel. Heidi gave a huge sigh of relief, following him as he led the way.

The past month had been a testament of her desire not only to reconcile the past with the present, but to find her way back to planning for the future. A future she hoped Kyle would play a role in.

But as she watched his tense shoulders and purposeful gait, she wondered if she'd waited too long. Had she lost him?

Yet she'd had no other choice. Life at the Joblowski house hadn't been all peaches and cream. But she was sticking it out, working things through with her mother and sisters, and finally understanding that it wasn't where you came from that mattered, but what you took from it. And in the process, she found she was much happier. Centered. She no longer felt pressured to put up a front she hadn't even known she had constructed to hide the teased and denied little girl who wanted so much to be included in what she'd believed to be "normal," and in the process had forsaken her own family.

Finally, she and Kyle reached the house. Heidi stepped into the kitchen, glad for the instant temperature change.

"You want something to drink?" Kyle asked in a tone that wasn't familiar. It was detached. Impersonal. And more than a little off-putting.

"Sure."

He washed up in the sink, splashing cold water over his face and then drying off with a nearby towel. Heidi watched the play of muscles down his back and took in the fit of his jeans against his backside. He caught her and she quickly dropped her gaze, unsure if her perusal was welcome.

He opened the refrigerator door. "I have beer, soda, lemonade…"

"Lemonade sounds great. My mom likes to say summer days like these are made for lemonade."

Heidi was surprised that she'd actually quoted her mother. Alice had been absent from her consciousness for so long, to have her back felt…strange, somehow. Yet also nicely familiar.

Kyle added ice to two glasses and then poured lemonade from a pitcher. He handed her one.

"Thanks."

He didn't respond as he half drained his own and then refilled it before putting the pitcher away. He watched her over the rim of his glass as he took another drink.

Heidi swallowed hard at the wariness in his eyes. He certainly wasn't making this easy on her. And perhaps it was no less than she deserved.

"So…" he said, putting his glass down.

"So…" she repeated.

"You said you had something you wanted to talk about."

She took refuge in sipping from her own glass, although she could barely force a trickle down her tight throat.

"I want you to meet my mother and sisters."

Kyle didn't say anything as he shifted his weight from one boot to the other.

"Can you please come sit next to me?" she asked with a nervous laugh.

"I don't think that's a good idea."

"Why?"

He lifted a brow as if to remind her of what had happened the last time they'd sat next to each other at that same counter.

But maybe that's what she wanted to happen again. She longed to go back to the way things were that night when she'd shown up at his door feeling as though the world had cracked in two and she needed help to superglue it back together. More importantly, he had helped her, without a thought or a moment's hesitation.

Now she had the sinking sensation that if she asked him for a Band-Aid he'd point her in the direction of the nearest pharmacy.

"So that's it? You came here to invite me to meet your family?" he asked quietly.

Heidi nodded, rubbing the condensation from her glass with her thumb. "Partially."

She felt his gaze go right through her as he apparently waited for her to elaborate.

"Are you seeing somebody?" she whispered without thinking the question through.

"What?"

"I don't know… You're acting so coldly I thought maybe…"

Kyle planted his hands on the counter and leaned against them as if trying to prevent himself from doing something he'd regret. "Do you have any idea of the hell I've been through over the past month, Heidi? A hell you put me through? For God's sake, I don't even want to take a shower now because I'm afraid if I leave the room, you won't be here when I get back."

She swallowed hard, unsure how to respond.

Finally, he pushed from the counter, crossing his arms.

"So that's it," he said. "You want me to meet your family."

She nodded. "Yes. I think once you do you'll understand a bit of what I've been trying to do over the past month."

Realization dawned that she should also recognize what he'd experienced while she was gone.

"And," she continued softly, "I want to start dating. Again."

His eyes glittered dangerously. "We never dated, Heidi. We had sex."

Of course, he was right. They had never dated. Worse, she'd been dating someone else during their trysts.

"Are you saying you want to ask me out?" His voice sounded a little kinder.

She blinked at him hopefully. "Yes."

His gaze flicked over her, leaving little forest fires in its wake. "When?"

Tonight, her heart screamed. "Whenever you're free."

"You're going to have to be more specific than that."

Heidi concentrated on the ice cubes melting in her glass. "I'm sorry, Kyle. I'm sorry if the past month hurt you. I...well, I had a lot of healing to do myself."

The hardness came back. "Your breakup with Jesse hurt you that badly?"

"What?" Her gaze snapped to his face. "No. I mean yes." She sighed heavily. "I mean, it did, but not in the way your tone seems to imply. Jesse was a big part of my life for a long time. But I'm more than okay that it's over. Our relationship had probably reached its end a long time ago, but neither one of us wanted to admit it."

She took a deep breath.

"By healing, I'm talking scars that go far deeper. Wounds that have nothing to do with Jesse…or maybe they do." She shook her head, still unable to communicate what she was going through in that area of her life.

She lifted her hands. "Look, I understand if you don't want to give this another go. It would probably be a good idea for us to take things slowly…"

"Slowly?"

She put her hands in her lap. "Yes."

"So when would you be interested in this date, then?"

She considered him standing on the other side of the island, looking wary and unsure, and wanted nothing more than for him to take her into his arms.

"How about tonight?"

Instantly he was beside her, doing exactly what she'd wanted him to.

Heidi hungrily kissed him, lapping the salt from his lips, his skin, restlessly running her fingers through his hair, pressing her needy body against his harder one.

Kyle groaned and stretched his neck back. "God, woman, do you have any idea how much I've missed you?"

"Do you have any idea how much you scared me just now?" she whispered. "I was afraid I was too late."

"I'm sorry. I just had to be sure."

"Of what?"

He searched her eyes and then grinned. "That this is what you truly wanted."

Her gaze flicked from his eyes to his mouth. Then she was kissing him all over again.

He chuckled. "So how slow are we talking about?"

"Screw slow," she said between uneven breaths.

He lifted her up into his arms and headed toward the stairs. "Best idea I've heard all day…"

Epilogue

Another month later...

IT WAS August and the late afternoon was hot and clear and promising for Nina and Kevin's wedding. Heidi had hired two high-school teens to help out so she might also fulfill her duty as maid of honor. But that didn't stop her from flitting around the tables, making sure everything was in order.

Kevin Weber's backyard was the perfect place for a wedding. Not so much because it was large, but his late mother had spent years tending to the hedge garden. A profusion of roses and perennials filled the space with color, the perfect backdrop for such an occasion, even with nearly a hundred and fifty of Fantasy's denizens milling about.

Kyle touched her arm and she turned to smile at him.

"You made it," she said, planting a lingering kiss on his lips.

He seemed to devour her with his eyes. She had changed at the house after finishing setting up the reception tables, so this was the first he'd seen her in the hot red number that Nina had chosen especially for her, insisting she wanted a dress that Heidi could wear again, not a pastel, fussy number that would end up gathering dust in the back of her closet while leaving a healthy dent in her savings account.

"Come here," she said quietly, spotting something on Kyle's right brow. "You've got a bit of paint on you."

He'd spent the past two days painting her mother's small house, where Heidi was currently living. Well, for the most part anyway. More and more often lately she was staying over at Kyle's place.

To look at her life now and compare it with two months ago was, well, not to recognize much of it. She was still catering. Still putting in hours, albeit shorter ones, at the BMC café. Still working toward her degree. But little else resembled the woman she'd once been.

And she was happier for it.

Kyle looked at his watch. "Shouldn't events be getting under way?"

Heidi noticed that the organist had begun playing music and that most of the guests had taken their seats. Kevin was standing at the end of a long aisle under a flower-covered arbor. He was looking at his own watch and tugging at the collar of his tux shirt.

Someone brushed Heidi as they passed.

Gauge.

She considered the man who co-owned BMC along with Nina and Kevin, but had disappeared in the midst of a hush of whispers six months ago. From the moment Heidi had first met him over a year ago, she sensed that beyond the handsome musician's easygoing style lay a dark, shadowy soul, and wondered if any woman would be able to paint it with light. When Nina had asked her a couple weeks earlier to help her look for him, to help her heal the rift between the three friends, Heidi had immediately accepted, wishing for things at the store to return to the way they had been. Before…before the three friends had tempted fate by becoming lovers…

Through, of all things, her mother's connections at the local pub and the musicians there, Heidi was able to find Gauge in Seattle, where he'd been sitting in with a local band. She'd been instrumental in convincing him to come to the wedding and had arranged for him to rent Jesse's sister Liz's garage apartment. But how long he planned to stay was anyone's guess.

Or, more accurately, would depend on how Kevin reacted to his return.

"He came." Heidi clutched Kyle's arm and they both watched as Gauge went to stand next to Kevin…

Heidi held her breath. She didn't realize how much she was hoping for a positive outcome until Kevin smiled, though his face revealed a shadow she'd never seen before. Still, he extended his hand. Gauge took it and they did the manly-handshake thing, complete with a half hug.

Heidi exhaled. While she didn't kid herself into thinking that all would be perfect from here on out, she couldn't help feeling that this was a good beginning.

It even looked as if Gauge was stepping up to act as Kevin's best man.

Heidi rested her cheek against Kyle's shoulder, giving a teary smile.

Kyle leaned down to whisper in Heidi's ear, sending shivers scooting everywhere. "You think there's time to…"

She moved to swat him in reprimand, but instead

found her hand squeezing his arm, reveling in the feel of his taut muscles beneath his suit jacket.

"Come on, you need to get up there." Nina's mother grasped her by the shoulders and maneuvered her toward the aisle.

Heidi hesitated, taking a moment to look into Kyle's eyes. Eyes that held love and desire and an emotional depth she planned on spending the rest of her life exploring. The thought filled her with sweet anticipation.

* * * * *

Wait! That's not it. Look for the conclusion of the **INDECENT PROPOSALS** *miniseries next month with Gauge's story,* RESTLESS...

Here is a sneak preview of
A STONE CREEK CHRISTMAS,
the latest in Linda Lael Miller's acclaimed
McKETTRICK *series.*

A lonely horse brought vet Olivia O'Ballivan to
Tanner Quinn's farm, but it's the rancher's love
that might cause her to stay.

A STONE CREEK CHRISTMAS
Available December 2008
from Silhouette Special Edition

———

Tanner heard the rig roll in around sunset. Smiling, he wandered to the window. Watched as Olivia O'Ballivan climbed out of her Suburban, flung one defiant glance toward the house and started for the barn, the golden retriever trotting along behind her.

Taking his coat and hat down from the peg next to the back door, he put them on and went outside. He was used to being alone, even liked it, but keeping company with Doc O'Ballivan, bristly though she sometimes was, would provide a welcome diversion.

He gave her time to reach the horse Butterpie's stall, then walked into the barn.

The golden retriever came to greet him, all wagging tail and melting brown eyes, and he bent to stroke her soft, sturdy back. "Hey, there, dog," he said.

Sure enough, Olivia was in the stall, brushing Butterpie down and talking to her in a soft, soothing voice that touched something private inside Tanner and made him want to turn on one heel and beat it back to the house.

He'd be damned if he'd do it, though.

This was *his* ranch, *his* barn. Well-intentioned as she was, *Olivia* was the trespasser here, not him.

"She's still very upset," Olivia told him, without turning to look at him or slowing down with the brush.

Shiloh, always an easy horse to get along with, stood contentedly in his own stall, munching away on the feed Tanner had given him earlier. Butterpie, he noted, hadn't touched her supper as far as he could tell.

"Do you know anything at all about horses, Mr. Quinn?" Olivia asked.

He leaned against the stall door, the way he had the day before, and grinned. He'd practically been raised on horseback; he and Tessa had grown up on their grandmother's farm in the Texas hill country, after their folks divorced and went their separate ways, both of them too busy to bother with a couple of kids. "A few things," he said. "And I mean to call you Olivia, so you might as well return the favor and address me by my first name."

He watched as she took that in, dealt with it, decided on an approach. He'd have to wait and see what that turned out to be, but he didn't mind. It was a pleasure just watching Olivia O'Ballivan grooming a horse.

"All right, *Tanner,*" she said. "This barn is a disgrace. When are you going to have the roof fixed? If it snows again, the hay will get wet and probably mold…"

He chuckled, shifted a little. He'd have a crew out there the following Monday morning to replace the roof and shore up the walls—he'd made the arrangements over a week before—but he felt no particular compunction to explain that. He was enjoying her ire too much; it made her color rise and her hair fly when she turned her head, and the faster breathing made her perfect breasts go up and down in an enticing rhythm. "What makes you so sure I'm a greenhorn?" he asked mildly, still leaning on the gate.

At last she looked straight at him, but she didn't move from Butterpie's side. "Your hat, your boots—that fancy red truck you drive. I'll bet it's customized."

Tanner grinned. Adjusted his hat. "Are you telling me real cowboys don't drive red trucks?"

"There are lots of trucks around here," she said. "Some of them are red, and some of them are new. And *all* of them are splattered with mud or manure or both."

"Maybe I ought to put in a car wash, then," he teased. "Sounds like there's a market for one. Might be a good investment."

She softened, though not significantly, and spared him a cautious half smile, full of questions she probably wouldn't ask. "There's a good car wash in Indian Rock," she informed him. "People go there. It's only forty miles."

"Oh," he said with just a hint of mockery. "*Only* forty miles. Well, then. Guess I'd better dirty up my truck if I want to be taken seriously in these here parts. Scuff up my boots a bit, too, and maybe stomp on my hat a couple of times."

Her cheeks went a fetching shade of pink. "You are twisting what I said," she told him, brushing Butterpie again, her touch gentle but sure. "I meant…"

Tanner envied that little horse. Wished he had a furry hide, so he'd need brushing, too.

"You *meant* that I'm not a real cowboy," he said. "And you could be right. I've spent a lot of time on construction sites over the last few years, or in meetings where a hat and boots wouldn't be appropriate. Instead of digging out my old gear, once I decided to take this job, I just bought new."

"I bet you don't even *have* any old gear," she challenged, but she was smiling, albeit cautiously, as though she might withdraw into a disapproving frown at any second.

He took off his hat, extended it to her. "Here," he teased. "Rub that around in the muck until it suits you."

She laughed, and the sound—well, it caused a powerful and wholly unexpected shift inside him. Scared the hell out of him and, paradoxically, made him yearn to hear it again.

* * * * *

*Discover how this rugged rancher's wanderlust is
tamed in time for a merry Christmas, in
A STONE CREEK CHRISTMAS.
In stores December 2008.*

Silhouette®

SPECIAL EDITION™

FROM *NEW YORK TIMES* BESTSELLING AUTHOR

LINDA LAEL MILLER

A STONE CREEK CHRISTMAS

Veterinarian Olivia O'Ballivan finds the animals in Stone Creek playing Cupid between her and Tanner Quinn. Even Tanner's daughter, Sophie, is eager to play matchmaker. With everyone conspiring against them and the holiday season fast approaching, Tanner and Olivia may just get everything they want for Christmas after all!

*Available December 2008
wherever books are sold.*

THE ITALIAN'S BRIDE

Commanded—to be his wife!

Used to the finest food, clothes and women, these immensely powerful, incredibly good-looking and undeniably charismatic men have only one last need: a wife!

They've chosen their bride-to-be and they'll have her—willing or not!

Enjoy all our fantastic stories in December:

REQUEST YOUR FREE BOOKS!

2 FREE NOVELS
PLUS 2
FREE GIFTS!

HARLEQUIN®

Blaze™

Red-hot reads!

YES! Please send me 2 FREE Harlequin® Blaze™ novels and my 2 FREE gifts (gifts are worth about $10). After receiving them, if I don't wish to receive any more books, I can return the shipping statement marked "cancel". If I don't cancel, I will receive 6 brand-new novels every month and be billed just $4.24 per book in the U.S. or $4.71 per book in Canada, plus 25¢ shipping and handling per book and applicable taxes, if any*. That's a savings of 15% or more off the cover price! I understand that accepting the 2 free books and gifts places me under no obligation to buy anything. I can always return a shipment and cancel at any time. Even if I never buy another book, the two free books and gifts are mine to keep forever.

151 HDN ERVA 351 HDN ERUX

Name	(PLEASE PRINT)	

Address		Apt. #

City	State/Prov.	Zip/Postal Code

Signature (if under 18, a parent or guardian must sign)

Mail to the **Harlequin Reader Service:**
IN U.S.A.: P.O. Box 1867, Buffalo, NY 14240-1867
IN CANADA: P.O. Box 609, Fort Erie, Ontario L2A 5X3

Not valid to current subscribers of Harlequin Blaze books.

Want to try two free books from another line?
Call 1-800-873-8635 or visit www.morefreebooks.com.

* Terms and prices subject to change without notice. N.Y. residents add applicable sales tax. Canadian residents will be charged applicable provincial taxes and GST. Offer not valid in Quebec. This offer is limited to one order per household. All orders subject to approval. Credit or debit balances in a customer's account(s) may be offset by any other outstanding balance owed by or to the customer. Please allow 4 to 6 weeks for delivery. Offer available while quantities last.

Your Privacy: Harlequin Books is committed to protecting your privacy. Our Privacy Policy is available online at www.eHarlequin.com or upon request from the Reader Service. From time to time we make our lists of customers available to reputable third parties who may have a product or service of interest to you. If you would prefer we not share your name and address, please check here. ☐

HB08R

Inside ROMANCE

Stay up-to-date on all your romance reading news!

The Inside Romance newsletter is a FREE quarterly newsletter highlighting our upcoming series releases and promotions!

Click on the <u>Inside Romance</u> link on the front page of **www.eHarlequin.com** or e-mail us at insideromance@harlequin.ca to sign up to receive your FREE newsletter today!

You can also subscribe by writing us at: HARLEQUIN BOOKS Attention: Customer Service Department P.O. Box 9057, Buffalo, NY 14269-9057

Please allow 4-6 weeks for delivery of the first issue by mail.

IRNBPA208

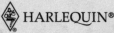

COMING NEXT MONTH

#435 HEATING UP THE HOLIDAYS
Jill Shalvis, Jacquie D'Alessandro, Jamie Sobrato
A Hunky Holiday Collection
Santa's finally figured out what women want—hot guys! And these three lucky ladies unwrap three of the hottest men around. Don't miss this Christmas anthology, guaranteed to live up to its title!

#436 YULE BE MINE Jennifer LaBrecque
Forbidden Fantasies
Journalist Giselle Randolph is looking forward to her upcoming assignment in Sedona…until she learns that her photographer is Sam McKendrick—the man she's lusted after for most of her life, the man she used to call her brother.…

#437 COME TOY WITH ME Cara Summers
Navy captain Dino Angelis might share a bit of his family's "sight," but even he never dreamed he'd be spending the holidays playing protector to sexy toy-store owner Cat McGuire. Or that he'd be fighting his desire to play with her himself…

#438 WHO NEEDS MISTLETOE? Kate Hoffmann
24 Hours: Lost, Bk. 1
Sophie Madigan hadn't intended to spend Christmas Eve flying rich boy Trey Shelton III around the South Pacific…or to make a crash landing. Still, now that she's got seriously sexy Trey all to herself for twenty-four hours, why not make it a Christmas to remember?

#439 RESTLESS Tori Carrington
Indecent Proposals, Bk. 2
Lawyer Lizzie Gilbred has always been a little too proper…until she meets hot guitarist Patrick Gauge. But even mind-blowing sex may not be enough for Lizzie to permanently let down her guard—or for Gauge to stick around.…

#440 NO PEEKING… Stephanie Bond
Sex for Beginners, Bk. 3
An old letter reminds Violet Summerlin that she'd dreamed about sex that was exciting, all-consuming, *dangerous!* And dreams were all they were…until her letter finds its way to sexy Dominick Burns…